THE GOD OF THAT SUMMER

Also by Ralf Rothmann

To Die in Spring

Ralf Rothmann

THE GOD OF
THAT SUMMER

Translated by Shaun Whiteside

PICADOR

First published in the UK 2022 by Picador
an imprint of Pan Macmillan
The Smithson, 6 Briset Street, London EC1M 5NR
EU representative: Macmillan Publishers Ireland Ltd, 1st Floor,
The Liffey Trust Centre, 117–126 Sheriff Street Upper,
Dublin 1, D01 YC43
Associated companies throughout the world
www.panmacmillan.com

ISBN 978-1-5290-0983-5

Originally published in 2018 as *Der Gott jenes Sommers* by Suhrkamp Verlag, Berlin.

1 3 5 7 9 8 6 4 2

A CIP catalogue record for this book is available from the British Library.

Typeset in Ehrhardt by Jouve (UK), Milton Keynes
Printed and bound by CPI Group (UK) Ltd, Croydon, CR0 4YY

I have looked upon this world and blessed it
For one day I encountered all the fear in the world.
If you count the days, I perished young.
But very old when you count the fear that I have felt.
Andreas Gryphius (1616–1664)

Reading, she lay on her bed and listened to the planes flying over the farm, trying to imagine what the snowy landscape with the canal must look like through the pilots' eyes. The winding cobbled road lined by fields and woods, the old ox track, led past the convent to Bovenau and divided the property in two. A steel bridge spanning the duck pond in a gentle curve led to the western side, to the white-washed manor house. Dominated by a portico on four columns – Doric, hollow plaster – it had a tiled roof and elegant arched windows which reflected the linden tree in the courtyard.

Opposite, the thatched roof of the big byre designed to hold three hundred cattle, with its hayloft, loomed higher into the sky than many of the local churches. Hanging from the gable was a bell which announced milking times, and the gate was decorated with shiny metal badges, awards from breeding associations and agricultural shows. On the side towards the field the machinery faced the farmyard; in it stood huge ploughs with shiny polished blades, tractors and an old hay-baler with stalks from last year's harvest still stuck to its spindle wheel. But of course the pilots couldn't see that, because the roof was undamaged. They had flown over the western part of the farm and the small park bordered by the Alte Eider behind the manor house, the first thing they looked down on was the dairy with its green glazed embrasures. The straw barn, a chicken coop for the poultry, various stables and a smithy were all on this side of the road. Some of the brick buildings, barely used now, were even older than the manor house and already becoming dilapidated. Each new attack ripped a bit more thatch from the roofs and laid bare the mildew-blackened walls or the nests of rats and martens.

Even though Kiel with its naval port was attacked repeatedly, not a single bomb had fallen on this farm which stood there unprotected, less than an hour's drive from the city, not during the whole of the war. An English Spitfire had once fired a round at the clock on the roof and destroyed the outside staircase leading up to the milkers' rooms above the byre, but to most pilots the landscape, with its softly rolling fields, the occasional smoking chimney, the stepped gable of the convent and the deer in the beech woods, must have seemed like the epitome of peace. No sign of a soldier, hardly a single military vehicle, and from their battered cockpits the men obviously couldn't see the underground bunkers or the camouflaged roofs of the sheds in the spruce forest – not to mention the U-boats that glided along the bottom of the canal towards the North Sea.

Once again it was long past midnight. Not a sound in the farmyard and in the attic room, and when all of a sudden wax dripped onto the page of the book, a clear pool beneath which the suddenly enlarged letters twitched like the legs of insects, Luisa blew the candle out. Immediately her room felt cooler, and she snuggled under her blankets, rubbed her feet with a yawn and thought for a moment she could see an afterglow of the little flame on the outlines of the furniture. A reddish rim shimmered on her water glass.

She got up, stepped into the eyebrow dormer and breathed on the frost crystals on the pane. No moon above the fields, only a few scattered stars, and still one could make out the trees along the thoroughfare, their black branches, and in the east there were flames behind a veil, impossible to tell whether mist or smoke. Either way, beyond it Kiel was burning.

*

The thin ice in the tractor tracks crunched beneath her soles when she went to the dairy the next morning. Carts and buggies stood along the Alte Eider, two dozen or more, and new ones were joining them almost every day. Some had sunk to the hub in the mud of the shore, their axles looming into the sky at all kinds of angles.

The sun was shining, but the wind on the ramp was bitter. Refugees with buckets, pots and jugs waited there, some of the women wore felt boots and several headscarves one on top of the other, and hardly anyone said a word. Everyone, even the children, stared at the door, where old Thamling busied himself with litre measures and quark scrapers. Luisa liked his bright, often teary eyes, his white sea-lion whiskers and his always benevolent 'It'll all come right! I'm sure it'll all come right.'

When he waved to her, past all the waiting people,

she was embarrassed. Milk was restricted, and the women at the back often went away empty-handed. She already thought she could hear grumbling; a toothless woman hissed something incomprehensible, a man on crutches, his thin jacket inflated by a gust of wind, reluctantly made way for her. The administrator grinned. 'Well, my girl? What's with the rings under your eyes? Latest fashion? You've been reading all night, haven't you? There was a light in your window.'

The lid of the dented aluminium churn was stiff. A note in her mother's handwriting fell out as it came away, a request for fat, and Luisa pulled her thick scarf, frosted from her breath, away from her mouth. 'Not the whole night!' she said. 'No more than a few hours.'

The administrator ran the ladle, with its handle as long as his arm, through the tiled basin. 'Still, I could see a light, a flickering candle, and the pilots will see it too, you know . . . Haven't you heard of blackouts? Man alive, I'd like to have your time. You can sleep and you don't. What are you on now?'

'*Winnetou II*,' she replied. 'But *Don Quixote* was better. I'll have finished *Treasure Island* by tomorrow, and next week I might start on *Effi Briest*. That story's supposed to be very sad . . . Did Kiel burn last night?'

He poured her some more milk, and when he pressed the lid down on the brimming jug, bubbles swelled out from beneath it. Then he pointed at the barrels outside the mosaic windows, the dog's empty treadmill. 'Say hello to your parents, but there won't be any butter again until tomorrow, Motte's paws are sore. And Kiel, or what's left of it, burns almost every night, my pretty. There's a war on, in case nobody's told you.'

She nodded awkwardly, thanked him and climbed carefully off the ramp. The angle irons on the steps were loose, and the administrator raised his head again and called: 'Luisa? Before you get back to your books, I'd be obliged if you would tell your sister to take her rumba shoes off in the flat. I can't stand all that trampling. Otherwise she can do the mucking out next time!'

Neither pulse nor breath, and yet it is life. We need only know what name to give it. But which writing stills the suffering of our days, which radiates into all the far-off times, which letter would be more than a stalk of hay beneath the hooves of the armies, who little know of justice though they murder in its name? The vanes hissed in the wind: the mill ground nothing but flames now, and sparks darted into the hay, laying waste the work of weeks in an instant. Bolts from crossbows pierced many a doublet, and anyone who resisted with stick or pitchfork, who wished to protect his most beloved possessions, had five warriors on top of him in an instant. The miller, his light extinguished by a blow from a club, twitched his last before his wife, and their children were hurled into the flames. The strangers shed great quantities of blood, it steamed in the frosty grass, and many died in anticipation, in fear, in fetters.

One of the tormentors, an officer with a blue feather in his hat, made the sheriff drink swill for the gold and where it was buried, and when he bit through the filling pipe they cut off his whereof-we-shall-not-speak while he was still alive. Another man, mighty as an ox, grabbed the man's daughter, who was a sister in holy orders and had come from Husum to consecrate the new chapel on the lake. He bound her tightly to the altar and beneath the cross he violated all her vows, whereupon the gentle creature lost her senses. She was found as good as dead, but she lived and returned to the convent, although no longer capable of singing. So the farm burned to the ground and all the cellars were empty, everyone lost the desire to live on the margins of the water, where the army's stragglers still roamed the Pikenwald, and other rogues too, filled with bloodlust and with greed. Stripped of all hope that times might get better, the village was filled with hot pouring tears and work was left undone. Many fields in need of care sank into weeds, and disputes grew among the ploughed fields where the bodies lay. The milk flowed sour from the cows, their calves died in the womb and, crazed with sickness and despondency, they walked as if in a bad dream.

Scarcely any news came out of the country, the only people who crept around were robbers, and they were beaten black and blue when they offered the corpses' jewels for sale. But there were single men who behaved lasciviously with a handful of women's hair, and a traveller came with finely woven bracelets and necklaces, so golden that the heart leapt with bliss in these dark days. He offered them to learned Bartholmes when he was about to set up his fishmonger's stall. And he recognized the string of pearls from the market in Lübeck, with the hair twisted around it. His wife, dragged off by marauders, was the only one far and wide who enjoyed such splendour and opulence, and the memory of his hands told him that the braid was his wife's. He fell dead into the water and the rogue made off.

The maker of these lines, Bredelin Merxheim by name, does not deem it appropriate to speak of his own suffering, for it is slight in comparison. Life is lived, one has chickens and rye bread in a stone house, and can read and write in spite of gout and cataracts, so one is well. If happiness smiles upon the valleys and endows us with fruits, no one thinks of sharpening one's quill, and parchment or hand-made paper are scarce. But if murder is on the road and the flames do their work and everything is levelled, there is still soot and oak apples aplenty for ink. So we shall continue with our chronicle and do justice to writing.

Only a few yearlings stood in the large byre now; the younger calves had been requisitioned. In their place the horses of the refugees were lodged there, the 'gypsy nags' as her mother called them. Apart from two black Trakehners most of them were brown, and the ravages of the treks, their hunger and exhaustion, were clearly apparent. The points of their hips and shoulders showed beneath their hides, dull and rubbed raw by collar and harness.

There was little for all of them to eat, a few armfuls of hay each day, and most of them were dozing or sleeping in their own dung when Luisa came down the corridor. But the mare that stood apart from the rest in the shade of the water tank already seemed to be waiting for her. The mare stared at her steadily from her sunken eyes, and her tail swept the wall. She was the thinnest horse of them all, her ribs could be counted, and she was also missing an ear. Unshod, she had pulled a big cart full of people and household belongings from Eastern Prussia to the Bay of Kiel, and now her joints were thickly swollen and her hooves looked like weathered timber.

Her coat was neither grey nor white, more a dirty yellow, and it was probably pain that made her lower lip with its sensitive bristles quiver. Blood ran from the cracks and abscesses that ran down her spread hoof, and the other horses repeatedly drove her away from the pile of hay; there were bites on her croup and neck. She wasn't even allowed to eat the old swallows' nests that fell from the walls or the roof-spars, and sometimes in her distress she cried out, a shrill sound. But the administrator had only shrugged when Luisa came running to him. 'Ah, the one from Kruschwitz . . . She's dying. And who wants to have death around the place?'

That morning the other horses approached, sniffing, when she clapped the sick mare – she had called her Breeze – on the neck with her hand. Some of them drew their ears back and kicked splinters from the brick floor with the tips of their hooves, and she closed a dividing fence and poured just enough milk into the trough so that no one at home would notice. Then she crumbled in some rusk as well, and suddenly she smelled the smoke and blinked into the sun's rays, which fell through the dusty windows.

'Well, take a look at that,' Sibylle said. 'Now I'm start-ing to get it!'

Her shadow slid across the whitewashed wall, where sheaves of straw were lined up. Her tightly tailored black coat with the astrakhan collar and high boots gave her an almost ladylike appearance – that and the fact that she was wearing her claret silk scarf, tied around her neck in a puff. In spite of the early hour, her lips were made up and her nails lacquered, and the open-worked gold earrings, a nineteenth-birthday present from her father, glittered in the sun.

'Where are you coming from?' Luisa asked, startled. 'Didn't you sleep at home? – And you're not supposed to smoke here. Everything could go up.'

Her sister, red-haired like herself and with the same curly hair, had, unlike her, dark eyes – a brown in which she seldom saw more than brown – and not nearly as many freckles. She flicked her cigarette ash on the floor. 'Oh, we're gradually getting used to that, plenty of experience by now. Of everything going up, I mean. But I think you're our guardian angel, even if you haven't got a halo. By the way, does the old man know what you're doing here? I remember that he doesn't like refugees in the stables . . .'

Luisa threw her scarf over her shoulder, stepped into the corridor and closed the gate. 'Why? After all, you're here too,' she replied. 'And besides, we're not refugees. We're from Kiel!'

Sibylle yawned. 'The things you say. And why did we leave Kiel? Could it be that it was getting a bit uncomfortable under our charred roof? In the air-raid shelter every night, that wasn't a dream, was it? So we packed our things and fled the bombs.' She scratched herself with her little finger beside her lip, where there was a birthmark, a tiny double dot: 'And what else do we call people who are fleeing, you little clever-clogs?'

Luisa felt herself blushing, a cool burning sensation. But her sister, who usually narrowed her eyes and triumphed coldly when she caught the twelve-year-old doing something nonsensical, didn't exploit her superiority this morning. She just laughed quietly down her nose, rummaged in her coat and held out a pack of 'Special Blend' cigarettes. She'd never done that before either. 'Luxury goods' it said on the label, 'sale on the open market forbidden!', and Luisa frowned. 'Keep them,' she said. 'You only want to butter me up so that I won't rat on you. And anyway, smoking's bad for you!'

There was the sound of tyres on the cobbles, and a squeak of brakes. Through the cobwebbed windows they could see a car with two soldiers in the back. The driver struck the horn and Sibylle grinned. 'The things you come out with. I've been wondering why my breathing whistles the way it does. But you know what's even more harmful? Always being serious and sensible, sweetie. That's the worst thing. It narrows your lips, gives you a poisonous expression, and even as a young thing you'll be quite old. Take a look at our stepsister.'

With the cigarette between her teeth, she pulled on her gloves, opened the door in the gate and stepped out into the street. 'So: if anyone's looking, I'll be a-cooking. And now please take the jug home and don't put water in it again! There's no sadder taste than diluted milk.'

*

She cycled through the forest to Bovenau. Several old linden trees had been felled by the shock waves from the bombs that a pilot had dropped here, even though there were no targets nearby; perhaps he wanted to shed his load before returning to base. Frau Thamling's bicycle was still a bit too big for Luisa, and she usually stood up on the pedals. It was only when the road went slightly downhill that she sat down on the saddle and brushed the hedgerow at the edge of the field with her boots. Then in the village the path was paved with gleaming cobbles and the lid of her bell rattled quietly as she turned towards the Simonis's farm.

The schoolhouse, which had also been where the teacher's family lived, was burned out, and the gable walls had collapsed in on themselves. Charred beams poked into the sky, lighter in colour where Herr Simonis had sawed bits of them off. He burned the pieces along with the thatch in the stove in the barn that had once been their classroom. Hanging on the wall was a swastika flag with a singed hem, and the teacher had also been able to rescue his lectern and the blackboard from the flames. The desks, however, had been destroyed; every child had to bring a chair or stool with them, taking them home again at lunchtime. Even a few months before, the classroom, where Herr Simonis taught all the classes at the same time, had been packed. But by now many of the pupils were deployed on field-hospital duty or as assistants to the anti-aircraft units, some as far away as Hamburg. This morning sitting at the roughly planed board desks were four girl evacuees, the two Kleber brothers in Hitler Youth uniforms and little Ole Storm. He had some coloured pencils and was drawing birds on a piece of cardboard when the teacher came down from the hayloft. The worm-eaten steps creaked.

With a picture of Hitler under his arm and his coat unbuttoned, as he did every morning, he wore his uniform jacket, two pairs of trousers of different lengths, a woollen cap with a brim and fingerless gloves. Since the aerial attack he lived with his young wife and their baby in a farm-hand's room beside the hay bales, and he was clearly still plagued by lice; at any rate he smelled of Goldgeist. He studied the children, nodded in response to their droning murmur of a greeting and hung the portrait on the wall. He had the same moustache as the man in the picture, a grey square. After they had sung the 'Horst Wessel' song he put on his old glasses, mended with tape, and asked to see the homework that most of them wrote on the framed slate panels that almost all of them used; there was hardly any paper left. Depending on the class they were fractions, declensions, geometrical drawings or handwriting exercises, and he marked them with his always sharp slate pencil; they could tell how displeased he was by how much it squeaked. The pupils in question had to stand bolt upright as he did so.

Little Ole, who sat next to Luisa, even clicked his heels together and placed his hands flat against his thighs. In spite of the cold he wore short trousers under his navy jacket, although with long socks. He had tied the straps of his cap under his chin, newspaper poked from his ankle-high shoes, and the teacher, a former trainer at the military school, sighed hoarsely. 'Damn it all, how often do I have to tell you, lad! You're nearly nine years old, you should be gradually mastering our language! So: all things that can be seen and touched are . . . ?'

He looked around, and one of the children, blonde Walburga with the pigtails, held her arm in the air and snapped her fingers. 'Written with capitals at the beginning, Herr Simonis. Because they are nouns.'

The teacher nodded. 'Did you hear that? You'd like to be a German boy, you want to join the Hitler Youth and the

Leibstandarte – and you can't get into your head something that even a girl can remember? An hour's detention!'

He crossed something out on the slate and pushed it so carelessly across the desk that a few coloured pencils rolled down and fell on the stone floor. The painted wood sounded as bright as glass, and ignoring the boy's sudden pallor, contorted lips and moist eyelids, he took a piece of paper from his lectern with writing on both sides and set it down in front of Luisa. It was her essay from the weekend. 'And now to us, my dear Fräulein Norff . . .'

But then Ole leapt to his feet again, wiped his eyes with his sleeve and sobbed: 'Of course, I've known that for a long time, Herr Simonis. Verb small, adjective small, noun big. Anything you can touch . . . House, herring, cup of cocoa. But Mimmi is quick as the wind, you can't catch her! She slips through your fingers like lightning!'

The laughter of the Kleber brothers, sons of the butcher in Steinwehr, sounded mocking, and tears dripped from Ole's chin when he sank to his knees to look for his pencils. One button of his sock-suspenders hung down, the skin between sock and trouser was marbled blue with cold, but the teacher didn't look up from Luisa's paper. 'Yes, yes,' was all he said, 'you lot are never short of excuses. Still, *Kätzchen*, a kitten, begins with a capital letter.'

'Van Cleef farm', it said on the handmade sheet of paper, a present from Herr Thamling, and the handwriting of her essay with the given title 'What I will do after the victory' looked as if it had been slightly smudged; the fibrous paper absorbed more ink than was needed for the individual words. Even so, the teacher seemed to have been able to read it all; he stretched out his little finger, pointed at the red-rimmed words and said: '*Amüsieren, flanieren, frittieren, Champagne* and *Portemonnaie* – now I'm wondering what language that might be.'

Luisa pushed a lock of hair behind her ear and looked at him uncomprehendingly. 'Yes, mine,' she said. 'No one helped me, I wrote it all myself. Only with the flower names I had to ask our Gudrun, she used to be a teacher. I always get rhododendron mixed up with wisteria and I never know whether snapdragons and hollyhocks are the same thing.' But all of a sudden she understood what he was getting at. 'Or do you mean,' she added in a softer voice, 'the foreign words? The words from the French?'

The teacher clicked his tongue. 'There we are, young lady, good morning! And who speaks that language?'

Luisa saw tiny reflections of herself in the convex lenses of his glasses and swallowed. 'Our enemies?'

Simonis opened the flap of the stove, pushed a log into the fire and poked it. 'Upon which you can bet your life. And now I shall find out, I am sure, what you were thinking, shall I not. Why do you use so many French words in an essay about the German victory, our richly deserved final victory? What links do you have with your worst enemy?'

Luisa, remembering that he had recently revealed the hiding place of two deserters, a hole they'd dug in the turnip pile, to the military police, took a breath, a quivering intake of breath. 'Me? Nothing at all . . . I mean, that's how we speak in my house. My father has a restaurant in Kiel, the officers' mess in the naval barracks, and he used to have one in Lübeck. Arms Minister Speer was there once and I

was allowed to eat his pudding, strawberries with cream.'
She swallowed. 'Isn't *Portemonnaie* correct?'

The wood was damp, it hissed and crackled, and the
teacher shut the flap. 'Blast it, no!' he shouted and threw
the poker into the corner. Dust trickled from the pitted
chalk-bowl by the board. 'In German we say *Geldbörse* or
Brieftasche! And we don't say *amüsieren*, we say *vergnügen*,
not *flanieren* but *spazieren gehen*, not *frittieren* but *braten* or
sieden. In good German Champagne is *Schaumwein*, *Coif-
feur* is *Frisör*, and your "*restaurant*" is not a restaurant,
Luisa, it is a *Gasthaus*, a *Schankraum* or a *Speisewirtschaft*.
You will be so kind as to write it all again! And sit down,
class six!'

His voice sounded strangely porous, hoarse and shrill at
the same time; the baby upstairs cried. Smoke puffed from
a chink in the stove door, the stalks hanging from the hay
loft began to tremble and suddenly, as if a cloudbank had
been penetrated all at once, they heard engines in the air,
the loud roar of a squadron swarming far over forests and
fields: 'Spitfires! Spitfires!' little Ole cried and leapt to his
feet. 'English planes!'

Luisa immediately pulled him back to his seat. The
teacher, who had just straightened the picture of Hitler,
whirled around; his eyes flashed with cold contempt.
'Nonsense, boy, how can you be so stupid! Those craven
corpses shun the light and come only at night, you know
that very well! They are afraid of our anti-aircraft units, the
famous gunners along the coast!'

The hum grew louder and the panes in the diamond-
shaped skylights vibrated in their frames; Simonis opened

the barn door a chink, and pushed his cap out of his fore-head. 'Excuse me: that's our own Luftwaffe, flying towards Berlin, the pride of the Reich Marshal. They are the courageous pilots who will sweep Germany free of all our enemies, and who knows, that may well be the advance party of the miracle weapon. Right everyone, outside! Wave with your caps, call out to them! Let us hail our victory!'

His wife came downstairs with the baby on her arm and looked at him, her eyes wide with fear. But he pulled the flag from the wall and, glad of the interruption of the class, the children jumped to their feet and followed their teacher across the yard and into the road. It was only when he reached the ditch at the edge of the field that he turned around, shielded his eyes and swung the flag. Red and white reflections glinted in the lenses of his glasses, and everyone except Luisa pulled their caps off and hopped up and down, waving their hands. She never wore a cap; she had thick hair.

The formations, apparently occupying the whole of the sky, were flying very high, just below the clouds; no inscriptions or insignias could yet be made out, at least not by the children. But the enthusiasm and the tears in the eyes of the teacher as he chewed his lip left no doubt about the allegiance of the planes. Blonde Walburga reached for a corner of the banner to wave along, and little Ole waved with both hands and cried, his voice almost breaking: 'Heil! Heil! Welcome, dear victory!'

The Kleber brothers stood stiffly, doing the Hitler salute, the older one correcting the angle of the younger's arm, and only when the roar of the bombers with the four propellers and glass noses was pierced by a different sound, a painfully shrill one, like the point of a compass being dragged along a blackboard, were their celebrations silenced. Far below the formations single-engine fighter planes appeared, a reinforcing escort painted with camouflage, and the circles on the fuselage and beneath the wings could clearly be seen: red, white and blue. Some were also painted with a crown.

Simonis silently moved his lips. The pilots wore leather helmets with built-in radio headphones and tinted goggles, and his eyes widened with astonished disbelief when a first round fired from one of the Spitfires struck the roof of the barn, which immediately started smoking. He pushed his glasses back, and his suddenly pale face turned into a grimace of horror. 'Take cover!' he yelled, bundled up the swastika flag and stuffed it under his coat. 'Run away, for God's sake! Run!'

A second salvo struck the pile of turnips at the edge of the field, shredded root vegetables flew across the farmyard and Luisa, who had thrown herself into the ditch beside the drive, covered the back of her head with both hands. Icy water ran into her shoes, something big and heavy struck her hard in the belly and she opened her mouth wide to catch her breath. But there seemed to be no air left, or if there was it only reached as far as her throat, like that time once in her garden in Kiel when the frail ropes of the swing broke. Feeling as if her chest and spine were paralysed, she breathed carefully in shallow gasps, because she felt it was impossible to take deeper breaths, or only at the cost of a burst artery or suffocating panic.

Once again a salvo was fired somewhere, distant cries, quiet whimpers. The smell of burning and urine rose into her nose, the warm, damp weight by her side grew heavier, and when she turned her head she recognized Ole, half covered by the cold earth. With blood on his ear, and his eyelids tight shut, he ran his tongue over his lower lip and whispered: 'Are we going to die now?' He crept closer to her, pushed his arms under her coat and pressed his cheek against her chest.

'No,' Luisa wheezed, now able to breathe in as if the air pressure had dropped. The engine noise faded away, and nothing could be heard now in the silence, not even the baby. She spat out some soil and plucked straw from the back of Ole's neck and buttoned his sock to its suspender. 'We're not going to die,' she said. 'It's over now.'

*

The next morning, when she came back from fetching milk, the kitchen was already warm. Her sister was crumbling turpentine soap into the pot that had formerly been used for making preserves, and from which vests and underpants now bulged. The water sloshed over the side as she stirred it with a wooden spoon, and a little way off some larger drops slid along the hot stove-top like quivering tadpoles before evaporating.

Luisa set the milk jug down on the table and unwrapped the butter from the paper, a page of the *Völkischer Beobachter*. The printer's ink had faded. 'Death before Capitulation!' it said in mirror writing in the grease, and she smudged the line with her finger and asked, 'Any news from Dad?'

Her nose wrinkled, her lips narrow, Billie pressed the washing deeper into the pot, and her brown eyes flashed in the fire that shone through the rings of the stove. 'If you hadn't blocked the whole luggage room with those books of yours there would still have been room for the tin of Persil and the powdered bleach,' she said, ignoring Luisa's question. 'How am I supposed to wash this stuff out with bloody cow soap? It barely foams and it smells like tar, and afterwards I'm going to get a rash or something!'

She had pinned her hair up with an amber comb, wearing nothing but a cream-coloured slip. Her forehead shone in the steam, and sweat ran from the dips in her collarbone, making the satin transparent in places. When she noticed Luisa's expression, she paused and looked down at herself. 'What is it? Why are you staring at my breasts?'

She licked her finger, the bluish fat that tasted a little like her paint box. 'No reason,' she said. 'Because they're so ugly. One of them is much smaller than the other.'

That might well have been true, but in fact Luisa thought they were very pretty, with the freckles at the top, their cheeky bounce and pale nipples, barely distinguishable from her skin; they lent her sister a delicacy that wasn't really hers. 'Rhett Butler would never kiss someone like you.'

A few days before when Luisa had crept into bed because of the cold, she had read to Billie from *Gone with the Wind*, the scenes with Aunt Pittypat. But Billie had gone to sleep and even snored. Luisa jumped aside when the wooden spoon came flying. 'Never!' she repeated. 'He has class, in fact, you . . . You're just scheming. Do you think I haven't noticed what you and Vinzent get up to, even right here in the flat? He's your brother-in-law!'

Her sister jutted her chin, knitted her reddish eyebrows and tried to look serious, but couldn't help giggling. Assistant to the Gauleiter and delegate to the Reich Food Authority, Vinzent Landes had since the start of the war been married to her half-sister Gudrun, her mother's daughter from her first marriage. They lived in a big house near Rendsburg, where there was even a bunker, and more or less as often as in his SS uniform – he was a Hauptsturmführer – he was seen in made-to-measure suits, even when inspecting fields and stables.

His late father, a half-brother of Admiral Dönitz, had left him the Landes tractor and thresher factory, in which cars were now being re-equipped for the front, underground, because the factories had been bombed to pieces. Sibylle laughed, a mocking sound. 'What do you know about class, bookworm? As little as you do about men. Poor Vinzent is unhappy, can't you see that? He's allowed himself to be bamboozled by the wrong woman. At the age of twenty-nine she talks as if she'd swallowed the Party constitution, and probably disinfects herself every time she . . .'

Their mother came into the kitchen. She was wearing the blue dressing gown with the purple cuffs and a tea towel as a scarf, and she put the hot-water bottle in the sink. Her sallow mouth was miserable, her cheeks sunken, and the line of her black dyed hair, pressed flat to the back of her head, was already reverting to grey. She didn't respond to her daughters' greeting, or only with a nod.

Her fingers trembled as she took a cup from the board

on the wall. 'What are you doing there, child?' she hissed and poured some coffee from the pot on the edge of the stove.

'Listen, don't leave the underpants to boil for so long. I don't want to spend all day stitching in elastic again.'

She slumped on her chair with a groan, and Sibylle, who had just been speaking in a hushed voice, almost through her teeth, straightened her back and said with a smile: 'I won't, Mummy dearest, you know me. I've just been soaking them. But I have to get the stains out at least. Are you still having headaches?'

Her mother closed her wrinkled eyelids and yawned, without holding her hand in front of her mouth; her lead fillings were clearly visible. Under her open dressing gown and her nightdress she wore one of the long pairs of knitted trousers that Luisa's father had sent them, raw wool and cotton mix from Wehrmacht supplies, and she scratched her knees. 'Oh, everything hurts, every single joint. It's almost unbearable. Gudrun absolutely has to get me some new tablets.' Then she poured some milk into the cup. 'Why is the jug only half full?'

Luisa gulped and gave her sister a menacing look. 'That was all there was left,' she lied. 'Too many refugees. And the forces take the rest. But we do on the other hand have butter, an extra ration with no ration stamps. We must have a pound! Have you heard anything from Dad? Kiel's been burning again, I could see the light from the flames!'

Holding the cup in both hands, her mother stared out of the window. 'Too many refugees,' she murmured. 'My God, where's it all heading; they're eating us out of house

23

and home. No country could bear that. And they're putting us up here, in a . . .'

But then she remembered her youngest daughter's question. 'How would I hear any news, poppet? There isn't a single working telephone left in the whole of bombed-out Kiel! But don't worry, nothing's going to happen to your beloved father. Nothing ever happens to him, he's got nine lives. He sticks his head in the oven and forgets to turn on the gas. And why should he care whether we poison ourselves with that revolting pump water or whether we die of consumption in this wretched shack, why should that worry him? The wind howls on the threshing floor, and my own shaking woke me up.' She looked at the table. 'Where are the cigarettes?'

Sibylle went over to the sideboard, rummaged in the drawer and put a white six-pack of Junos on the table. 'I think those are the last ones,' she said with surprise. 'I could have sworn . . . Well, what's to be done. If you need some, I've still got a few Special Blend. Vinzent should be bringing some more.' She lit her mother's cigarette, and Luisa opened the misted window and set the milk jug outside.

'But how can you say Dad does nothing!' she protested. 'We've got nearly everything we need, we can boil the water, and if there was any coal left he would have installed a heating system long ago, the burner is in the stable. Is it his fault if it doesn't work with wood?'

Her mother said nothing. She drew on her cigarette, threw back her head and closed her eyes, a sign for Sibylle. The girl wiped her hands on her petticoat and raked her mother's dull hair from her forehead. Then she rubbed her ears between her fingertips and gently massaged her temples, which made her groan out loud as she only normally did in the bath. 'Oh, yes, that feels lovely, my darling. You do that wonderfully well, wonderfully well. I'd like to be a man in your hands!' Expelling the smoke through her nose, she twisted her eyes and looked behind her. 'By the way . . . How do you know that handsome Vinzent still has supplies?'

Her mother bulged her cheek with the tip of her tongue, and Sibylle let her delicate fingers wander over her scalp like spiders' legs. 'Well, don't concern yourself. He understands that he needs to deliver them, he can put two and two together,' she murmured, and pulled a face at her sister. 'And if he really hasn't got any, he's getting nothing more from me. And the sweetshop will be closed to Herr Sturmführer. I've got cystitis again anyway.'

Then their mother laughed, a raw sound, almost like a cough, and pinched Sibylle's breast. The girl recoiled with a shriek, and Luisa picked up her coat and scarf from the chair and went to the door. 'By the way, if we've lost the war and the Asiatic hordes are on the way,' she said casually, 'they'll shoot the capitalists first. A refugee woman from Silesia told me that, she still had blood on her shoe. And we'll be brutally raped – Mama, Gudrun, Billie, everyone. Scratch your mouths raw, because then they'll think you've got syphilis and they might leave you alone.'

For a moment the only sound was the crackle of firewood, the simmering of water in the pot, and, already in the corridor, she stuck her head into the kitchen where the women were staring at one another, both suddenly grey as lye. 'But only maybe!'

*

The convent gardens began about a kilometre east of the farm. The plain main building, brick Gothic, was topped by a tower and had a small cloister overlooking the Alte Eider, full of roses in summer. For now it served as a field hospital for officers, and the Carmelites had been ordered to brick up the cross on the stepped gable, a shadowy niche – and they had done so with brand-new bricks.

Luisa leaned her bicycle against the fence and untied the basket from the luggage rack. Frau Thalming had filled it to the brim with eggs, layer after layer resting on straw, and clearly none of them had got broken on the way along the cobbles, nothing was dripping from the mesh. She went to the courtyard door, in which there was a hatch for food for the poor, and pulled the chain; the bell inside the building was silent, and her knocking went unanswered.

She pushed down the latch. There was nobody in the kitchen in the basement arches. Big pots and pans full of toast stood on the edge of the stove, which was fed by pine cones. Not one moved when a rat crept into the big pile below the window, and Luisa set the basket on the table and looked into the corridor and called for the cook. Sister Mathilde, a little hunchbacked woman who had run the convent since the arrest of the prioress, was nowhere to be seen.

Books in boxes were stored in the utility rooms, stacked up to the ceiling, because like most of the cells, the print room, the sewing room and the refectory, the library was also being used as a sick bay. Beds, more beds and bunks had been cobbled together from the old writing and reading desks and the oak boards of the shelves. Every week army ships appeared from the east in the Bay of Lübeck, and often wounded men who had abandoned hope died in the basement corridors. Blood-stained mattresses leaned against the walls.

Luisa slowly climbed the stairs to the ground floor, the smell of chloroform becoming stronger with each step. Clothes, boots, newspapers and canteens hung on lines under the corridor ceiling, and soldiers lay everywhere, even in the foyer and the prayer room. From all the cells and the gallery came the groans, whimpers and screams of the young men, metallic clattering, sharp clicks and once a curt 'Stop making such a fuss!' Somewhere a radio was on, Willy Birgel singing songs from operettas.

Some sunlight pierced the skylights, gloomy rays. A uniformed doctor limped cursing along the floorboards and looked at his watch. His left leg was stiff, a metal rail made every step sound as if he were hammering nails into wood. The nurse who followed him with a tray full of phials and syringes paused and came to a standstill. It was Sister Mathilde. 'Hello, Luisa, what are you doing here?' she said quietly. 'Has something happened?'

Like all the nuns in the convent, she had had to swap her veil and flowing brown habit for the grey uniform of the German Sisterhood. She hurried down the corridor, and the girl reached into her coat pocket. 'No, nothing in particular. I just wanted to say that there's a basket of eggs in the kitchen, with best wishes from Frau Thamling; they're today's, four dozen, I assume. And I also managed to get hold of this.'

The woman opened her mouth, widened her eyes dramatically and put the tray down in a window niche. There were fingermarks on her white skin, and the lenses of her glasses were sprinkled with brown stains. 'Peacetime wares? I can't believe it! How did you manage to get this?' she whispered and picked up the pack of Junos. 'I'm sure you can't get those on ration cards, can you? Oh, child, you know how to gild an old woman's day.'

She tapped out a cigarette, sniffed it and rummaged for a lighter from her apron. With her eyes closed, however, she took only one drag and groaned with pleasure; then she bent down and placed it between the lips of a wounded man with thickly bandaged arms. He puffed on it greedily, and she ran the backs of her hands over the girl's cheek. 'Thank you, my love, I'll pay you back. We'll be going through the books shortly. Now you get off home. You'll only get bad dreams here.' She took the tray out of the niche and followed the doctor, and Luisa was about to go too – when she felt herself being gently held back. One of the soldiers was tugging on the hem of her coat, and looking up at her. Seagrass spilled from his uncovered mattress. 'Please, sister, help me!' he murmured, and he sounded dazed, as if he had just been sleeping. 'I can't sit up. There's something wrong with my back.'

A man of about forty, he had a wide bandage over his chest, and his elbow had been punctured in several places. Plainly he hadn't been washed, let alone shaved since being wounded at the front. The place where his helmet strap had been was clearly visible on his sooty cheek. His lips were chapped, his teeth coated, his fingernails black, and Luisa gave a start when she discovered his true age from the case notes on the wall. She bent over him and said, 'I'm sorry, Herr Neumann, I'm not a nun. Shall I call one of them?'

The man closed his hollow eyes. 'No one will come,' he answered hoarsely and felt for his neck, the identity disc on the little chain; the rims of his eyelids were moist, his nostrils twitched. 'They never come. They leave you here for hours in your uniform trousers, everything itches with lice, and my feet hurt so much. Can't you at least take my boots off, sister? I can't do it on my own!'

Luisa nodded. She took a newspaper photograph of Ilse Werner and some letters off the eighteen-year-old's bed and put them all behind his pillow. It was a bag full of seed husks, and no sooner had she pulled back the ragged field blanket, devoured by moths or rodents, sending thick dust billowing through the sunlight, than a rotten smell reached her. Retching, she raised a hand in front of her mouth. At first she thought that the man had simply emptied his bowels. But what looked at first sight like excrement was tattered or lacerated paper bandages, rusty brown with dried blood, bright red with fresh blood. His legs had been amputated more or less from the spot that his boot tops would have reached. Now pus ran from the stitches, which had been prepared very roughly, with thick yarn, and for a moment she was reluctant to make the connection, it was impossible. But there was no getting around it. The stumps looked like tied sausage ends.

29

She felt dizzy, and swallowed down her spittle and pulled the blanket over the sight, her hands trembling. Not knowing what to say, she raised her hands and breathed deeply. But the boy, whose dog tag was broken along its perforation, a semi-oval, seemed to have gone back to sleep. Tears had left pale traces on his dirty cheeks, his lower lip twitched as he began to snore, and Luisa straightened up completely, linked her fingers together and whispered a prayer, a quick, 'Help him! Please help!'

Like all images of the Madonna or the saints, the cross on the wall at the end of the corridor had been taken down on the orders of the authorities, but the shape of the dust still revealed where it had once hung.

*

Her father usually came in the dark, with his headlights dimmed in line with regulations. But when the moon was brighter over the canal the black car could be seen driving off the ferry. That was how it was tonight too, and she slipped into her coat and ran from the flat without saying anything to the others, who were listening to swing records in the sitting room. In the stairwell, below the old hunting pictures and antlers, she always took two steps at once, opened the heavy front door and waited for the Mercedes to turn off the main road.

The courtyard with its old linden tree was half in the shadow of the byre. It was cold, not a soul to be seen. Frost glittered on the mossy thatch and the ridge turrets with the animal heads. On the other side of the road, behind the lancet windows of the dairy, a rhythmic squeak could be heard. Fastened to the old treadmill, Motte, Thamling's old butter-dog, trotted as he tried to snap at the piece of fur or venison that hung unattainably close in front of his snout. A series of axles and cogs connected to the flywheel turned the cranks which in turn rotated the beaters in the barrels. And they beat the cream until it was solid.

Somewhere Luisa heard giggling, and she narrowed her eyes to see more clearly. Instead of the ruined steps outside, a long ladder rested along the wall of the byre; whoever was climbing down it rung by rung, often treading on the hem of his coat, it wasn't one of the young men who lived in the warm rooms above the byre. Always impatient or late or both, they pressed their heavy, milk-fat-polished boots against the spars and hurtled like firemen into the courtyard.

One of them, a fair-haired boy with clear blue eyes who always had a cigarette in his mouth, even owned books, a little shelf of them. Luisa once had to bring tablets to his room when he had a fever, and by the light of the paraffin lamp he had read her something by a writer with a woman's name, Maria Ricke or something. 'The Stranger' was the name of the poem, and she had found it barely comprehensible, mysterious. Still, the finely tuned sounds and the melody of the words had moved her so much that tears had come to her eyes.

Because no one else climbed down that ladder, her sister giggled again, and the man under the cantilever roof whispered to her to be careful. His face was pale and there were dark circles around his eyes, his hair was tousled, he wore striped pyjama trousers and a tight T-shirt, and even though his shoulders were quite narrow, his chest and arm muscles seemed quite pronounced, as if moulded by the moonlight. When Billie was finally standing in the court-yard, she blew him a kiss, but he tapped his forehead and closed the door.

With the astrakhan collar of her coat open, she walked around the linden tree and hummed a tune. Her high, nickel-plated heels rang out on the cobbles as if she were walking on glass, and although Luisa had stepped towards the pillar of a portal in the shadows and held her breath so that she didn't give herself away with a cloud of condensa-tion, her sister spotted her. 'Alone out at night, my pretty child?' she asked, clearly not surprised. Her smile looked weary and rested at once. 'Are you sleepwalking, or waiting for your lover?'

Luisa didn't answer at first, she looked over towards the entrance to the courtyard, the broad bridge over the moat. The steel railings, a stylized weave of plant-like forms, were white with frost. Luisa was uncomfortable with the idea that Sibylle might be there when she threw her arms around her father, not having seen him for so long. She wanted to be alone with him, at least for a few minutes, and said as dismissively as possible, 'What about you? I thought you were listening to records with Mum. What are you doing up there in the milkers' rooms? Does she know?'

Her sister reached behind her head and rearranged her curls. 'Oh, so they're milkers? That'll be it . . .' she mur-mured, with a hairpin in her mouth. 'Yeah, the things we get up to with them. Just messing about, of course. Do you know what the milkers call the League of German Maidens? The League of German Mattresses.'

If that was a joke, Luisa didn't understand it, and she didn't react. Her sister, leaning against a pillar, folded her arms and breathed deeply. She smelled of alcohol, the cheap Kümmel that the workers always drank straight from the bottle. A screech owl called in the trees in the park. 'Spring's not going to come, is it? Nothing blooms, nothing smells nice, nobody's in love. It's all down to this damned war, it's paused time. I can hardly remember not being cold.'

She dabbed something from her lip, studied her fingertip and wrinkled her nose. Then she smiled again and said, 'When there's a full moon I'm always wide awake and full of beans, aren't you? It's like being under a spell: I bleed and can't get to sleep. In Kiel or Lübeck I could at least wander around the houses, stroll through the ports with the sailor-boys. But in this godforsaken place there's nothing but wet meadows. Why do you think Dad comes to visit? That's why you're standing here, isn't it?'

Luisa shrugged. 'I saw the car on the ferry, a while ago,' she said. 'He's coming more and more rarely, isn't he? It's a month now since the last time. Do you really think he would do something like that again? The thing with the gas stove I mean.'

Her sister grunted quietly and waved dismissively. 'Nonsense, that was all play-acting!' she answered. 'He loves life more than you love your books. He probably just wanted to be rescued. Mama isn't exactly a cuddly toy.'

Luisa nodded. Even though it had happened years ago,

she couldn't shake off her anxiety. Even in the garret where there was only a wood-burning stove, she sometimes started from her sleep because she thought she smelled gas. But it was probably the slurry that never quite congealed, behind the stables.

For a while she listened into the night; no engine noise, not even in the distance. Clouds striped the moon and the squeaking noises from the dairy fell silent. Motte seemed to be resting, or else the butter was solid, and she tapped the tip of her shoe against the foot of the pillar, which rang hollowly, cleared her throat and asked, 'What's it like to be raped? What do they do exactly? Does it hurt a lot?'

A screech owl flew across the yard, close to the ground, almost touching the shadows of its wings, and her sister actually paused and looked at her for a moment, bewildered; but contrary to Luisa's expectation no mockery appeared on her face, nothing frivolous, more of a faint melancholy that played around her sprightly lips. 'I'm sorry? What's up with you? I thought you were only interested in poetry and animals,' she said, and touched her necklace, the pierced river pearl, moving it slowly back and forth. 'What made you think I might know that?'

Luisa hunched her shoulders. 'Just,' she said, embarrassed. 'Do you think the Silesian woman was serious about scratching your mouth because of syphilis? Do they leave you alone if you do that?'

She had been whispering involuntarily, and Billie laughed bitterly and said at her normal volume: 'Well, I wouldn't bank on it. Those lads are so hot for female flesh – they couldn't care less whether you have diseases or not. They'll be dying soon themselves . . .'

She fell silent for a while and wiped her sleeve, the fur cuff, against the big buttons of her coat. They were covered with fabric and had a slightly worn sheen.

'Yes, it probably does hurt,' she murmured. 'A lot. But don't scream, don't struggle and don't go rigid or they'll break all your bones. At least that's what I've heard. It's best to turn your head away, shut your eyes and think it will pass, like everything in life. What are you supposed to do? They're the strong ones. Everything passes . . .' She looked up with a sigh. 'Well, excuse me, here comes the apple of your eye, unless I'm very much mistaken.'

The black car had turned into the courtyard almost silently, but Luisa, who would on any other evening have jumped from the steps and held her arms outstretched to greet her father, remained frozen in response to what she had just heard, which she could only vaguely imagine – and which made it even stranger. It was dark inside the Mercedes, it seemed bigger than last time, and when she noticed the folding roof and the spare tyre at the rear, she shook her head with disappointment. And of course her father didn't have SS runes on his number plate. 'No,' she said, 'it's not him.'

The headlights under the rubber hoods went out, and two men in unbuttoned uniform coats crossed the courtyard and studied the facade of the manor house, the high windows. They didn't say a word of greeting, a nod at most, and while one of them stepped into the foyer and knocked at the administrator's door, the other pulled the gloves off his fingers and ran his hand over Luisa's hair. As he did so, however, he studied her sister, looked her up and down through his rimless glasses and said, 'What's up, girls? Shouldn't you be tucked up in bed?' His tongue slid over his lower teeth. 'Or does it get a bit lonely in there?'

An aluminium fibre cord and a death's head gleamed on his cap, and the girl he had addressed didn't reply, or only by briefly closing her eyelids in apparent reflection. She held her astrakhan collar together under her chin, sucked in her cheeks a little and looked into the sky for a moment. The stars glittered icily. 'Good evening to you too!' she said at last, making her voice sound darker than it really was, and the officer went into the house with a grin. The door slammed shut.

The shutters came down in the landowners' flat. On the other side of the courtyard the treadmill could be heard again, the butter-dog in the dairy. Lately he had been wearing leather cuffs on his paws. Billie stepped out of the shadow of the portico, straightened her silk scarf and said, 'Right, then, people. Sleep well, sweet dreams.' She bent her fingers and studied her painted nails. 'I'm off to howl at the moon for a bit.'

*

Her father only turned up a week later. It was night again, the floorboards creaked, the strip of light under the door twitched with shadows, and she jumped out of bed. Hanging in the corridor, where the pendulum of the grandfather clock gleamed, was his heavy coat, its fabric still cool. It smelled of Flor del Arte, his favourite cigars, and as she walked in her pyjamas along the worn linoleum, she tried to make out what was being said in the kitchen.

Her mother was shouting, that much was plain. Paper was crumpled, the cutlery drawer was shoved violently back into the cupboard. She was speaking very quickly, each word more breathless than the last, and her voice assumed the hoarse quality that was often a harbinger of tears. Luisa's father, on the other hand, remained calm, and the sound of his soft yet sonorous voice wrapped something velvety around her soul: 'Oh, balderdash,' he said. 'Where did you get that idea? Nobody's going to take these rooms away from you.'

The tar paper, printed with roses, felt cool on the feet. She opened the door, pretended to yawn and rubbed her eyes before stepping into the overheated kitchen.

The lamp hung low and logs crackled in the oven; her mother leaned against the bar of the stove. With her hands in the pockets of her dressing gown and paper curlers in her hair, she twisted her mouth in disapproval and said, 'What's all this? It's past midnight, I hope you're on your way to bed!'

But her father, wearing his dark gabardine suit with the light grey waistcoat that covered his stomach, smiled broadly. His high forehead gleamed, as it usually did when he drank, the whites of his eyes were quite red and after they had hugged and kissed he held her tightly by the shoulders with his slightly swollen hands and looked at her emotionally. 'My innocent little love! You get bigger by the month,' he said at last. 'I hope we didn't wake you?'

She shook her head and glanced at the table, the bottles,

tins and boxes on it – no Danish sherbet powder this time, apparently, no chocolate – and pressed herself against him again. 'No,' she said, now really yawning, and holding the backs of her fingers in front of her mouth. 'Knowledge never sleeps, Papa.'

That was a phrase that he usually used when she read too long at night, and he wrapped his arm around her waist with a chuckle and turned back towards his wife. His shirt collar was wrinkled, a wooden stay poked from the tip, and there was a stain on his tie. 'Believe me, Gerda, if even Vinzent's hand are tied, the administrator really won't be able to do anything,' he said. 'They'll soon be packing his flat full of people as well. And the rooms at the end of the corridor are still empty. You'll share the kitchen and the bathroom for a while, and then it'll all be over anyway. They'll be officers' wives and their children, which means they'll be clean people. They won't be pissing on the toilet seat.'

Now her mother clicked her tongue and glared at him as she always did when he used street talk in front of his daughter or used obscene language. He waved a reassuring hand. 'Yes, fine! *Pardonnez-moi*. I'm from Dithmarschen,' he said. Pearls of sweat glittered at his hairline. 'You know what that means, don't you?'

She rolled her eyes and opened a skylight. Luisa couldn't bear to listen any longer and studied the objects on the table more closely. Her father had brought several bottles of Bols liqueur and red wine, brightly printed tins of tea, cocoa and coffee beans, a fat cervelat sausage and a stone pot full of fish paste with capers. There was also a round loaf of rye bread and another of raisin bread, a big box of smoked mackerel and a small bag of hazelnuts. 'Take it all,' he said with wave of his hand. 'This is my body, this my poor blood that I have shed for you.'

A gurgle came from the groundwater pump beside the sink, and Luisa kissed his temple and murmured close to his ear: 'Thanks, Dad, you are so kind! Did you remember my books as well?'

Frau Mangoldt, an old neighbour who had recently died, had left her a whole shelf of them, and he nodded gravely. The light shone through his thin hair. 'Naturally, *dottoressa*. The box room is crammed to the gills with them. We'll clear it out tomorrow morning.'

He poured himself another cognac and offered some to his wife, but she shook her head; as far as she was concerned the conversation wasn't over. 'Now please give it some thought!' she said, and pulled a light blue pack of cigarettes out of her pocket. 'If that shower of Standarten-führers or Sturmführers or whatever they are move in here with their pictures of Hitler or Himmler, and the Russians come, they might think we're an SS family! They won't give a damn about whether we have a Party membership card or not, and they won't give it a second thought! They'll have us all against the wall or send us to Siberia!'

She tapped a Gold Dollar against the back of her hand, looking as if she was making a series of little exclamation marks in the air, and with a wink her husband flipped over his lapel. Membership of the Nazi Party had been a condition of the lease on the officers' mess, but he always kept the 'bonbon', the Party badge, hidden. 'Yes, I know!' she said and waved dismissively. He pushed his lighter over to her. 'Calm down now, Gerda, the Russians aren't coming, that much is certain. The British might, on the other hand . . . But they're civilized, they're scared of women; you have nothing to fear from them.'

She frowned, turning the painted arcs of her brows into two crooked snaking lines, and exhaled smoke under the lamp. 'Oh really? So you're better informed than the radio, or how do you know so much about it?'

He sniffed the cognac and took a sip. 'Because I know, my darling. Because I was an admiral's steward and I run an officers' mess in a barracks; you hear certain things that aren't intended for everyone's ears. If I could turn that into money . . . Look into the sky, who's shooting at us and bombing us here in the north? The Americans, the French or the Russians, perhaps?'

'No,' Luisa said, 'it's the English. Spitfires. They hit our school as well.'

He licked his lips. 'Exactly so! The country has been divided for a long time. The Soviets will come no further than Wismar, and they can have that dreary hole. There may be a bit of noise here and there, I'm sure the last bomb hasn't fallen, and perhaps a few old men will have to join the Volkssturm, but all in all we will . . .'

The hinges of the door squeaked and he fell silent, and a vertical line appeared over his nose. But then he loosened his tie and said, 'Well hello, this is a sight for sore eyes!'

Sibylle came into the kitchen, also wearing her dressing gown. The holes in her earlobes were empty, her hair tied back, there was a thick layer of vanishing cream on her forehead and cheeks, and she hadn't removed all her make-up; there were black lines around her eyelids. She wore thick woollen socks, at least two pairs, and while she was kissing her father, she gently pinched Luisa's bottom and moaned, 'Do you have to make so much noise?'

Yawning, she sank into the wing chair in the corner. There were also tiny traces of lipstick in the corners of her lips, and she drew her feet up under her bottom and gave her mother a sign with two fingers. Her mother threw her the cigarettes, and when she reached for them, her floral-patterned gown opened and revealed a new petticoat, white silk with red piping below the breast. 'Well, Mr Tearabout? What's going on up at the coast, how's Kiel?' she asked, and struck a match. 'Still got sprats up there?'

Luisa knew she wasn't really interested. It sounded more as if she wanted to distract her father from the sight of her painted nails, her expensive underwear and the blue mark on her neck. He also didn't like to see her smoking. Still, he pushed the ashtray towards her.

'Well, at least you can be very glad that you live here in the country,' he said, and rubbed his tired eyelids. 'Imagine a big pile of rubble and bricks with a few arms and legs sticking out of it, that's Kiel. Everything smells rotten, it's amazing that there are still people in the ruins. But again and again they climb out of the burnt holes, dust themselves down and try to get some water or a piece of hard bread until the next attack. As a young man in the first war I didn't see as much blood and misery as I am seeing now in my own homeland.'

Luisa, half-sitting on his lap, wrapped both arms around

his neck, pressed her nose against his cheek and asked: 'Then why are you still there?' She loved his aftershave, the smell of pine trees, witch hazel and a hint of menthol in the morning. But in the evening he smelled only of tobacco and alcohol. 'Stay with us! School's been closed down because of the low-flying planes, and you could teach me!'

Again he uncorked the bottle. 'Yes, that would be nice,' he said and bit back a yawn. 'I'd really love that, child. But there are a few hundred sailors and officers who I have to keep supplied, not counting the gentlemen from the security service. I've signed contracts. What do you think they would do with you if I . . . That would be subversion of national defence!' He ran his hand over her head. 'But don't worry, nothing's going to happen to me. The city and the harbour are in ruins, but not a single bomb has fallen on the naval barracks, not a splinter.'

He looked at his wife, took a sip and said into his cognac glass: 'And you know why that is, Gerda? Have a think!' But she waved the question away and Billie asked: 'Because the English can't aim?'

He didn't smile. 'No,' he said. 'Because they're intelligent. They know exactly what to destroy and what not. The farms with the dairy cows, the big railway bridges near Rendsburg and the barracks in Hamburg-Langehorn have been carefully spared. Soon they'll be wanting to move in there themselves, you see. Who's going to want to bomb the supply routes or their own beds out from under their arses! Where are they supposed to take their little strumpets when they celebrate their victory?'

Billie laughed, a bright sound, and pulled her dressing

gown across her chest, and Luisa couldn't help chuckling as well, because she liked the word, and imagined brightly tootling musical instruments. But her mother hissed: 'Willi, that's enough!'

She stubbed her cigarette out on the hob and threw the butt into the empty coal scuttle, and he opened his light brown eyes wide and raised his hands in a pacifying gesture. 'All right, that's fine. I apologize for my choice of words. I'm a simple soul, children, an ordinary person from Dithmarschen. Endless cabbage fields, eternal rain. And you know that *Dith* is Plattdeutsch and means cow dung, and *Marsch* means land. You know that, don't you?'

Billie closed the skylight, and Luisa awkwardly twisted a pyjama button. Even though no one could bear to hear it, he almost always said it when he was drunk. When he got to his feet he bumped into the lamp. 'So however cultured I might be: I come from Dungland,' he went on and grinned at his wife. 'Of course I would rather it was called Rosewater Dale; but its real name is Dungland, and I only really wanted to say that you don't need to go wetting yourselves over the Russkies.' Then he slapped Luisa on the bottom and growled: 'Right, time for bed.'

That in happiness guilt also lies, but in suffering mostly innocence: this knowledge has sometimes been a nourishing source of comfort for the author of these lines, tormented as he is by raging hunger. Sorrow made his hand tremble, but even in spiritless times writing must be done as testimony for future generations, so that man may become wiser and more clear-sighted. He should not direct his innermost soul towards the sharp blade of greed and the noise of battle, but towards meekness, as it dwells in women, and the sound of silence that is louder than the voice of our Lord.

The misery was all-consuming and became still greater with each new army of hirelings that burned its way through the land and claimed tributes for life and right of way. Everything had to go into the street, every pot, every sock, mirror, bed and chair. The wells were poisoned, in the barns nothing but wind, we ate grass and tree-bark like cattle. At the wayside were corpses enough to still our hunger with liver and spleen and anything the teeth could tear. At night Kontradin the tanner went forth and broke the bones with his axe, and the whimpering people followed him like rats, and swallowed and choked and begged the Lord for forgiveness with their bloody mouths.

But there were plagues, also, pestilence and Hungarian fever, brought to our houses by lansquenets and refugees. And indeed the author of these lines was not spared; mad with brainworm and red with roseolas he lay for weeks in the care of his maid who had been many times dishonoured and even called her mother and saint. But she knew herbs and had patience.

Even more than hunger, plagues and fear of barbarians, of any flag, grief and black bile ate away at people, the vision of a heaven that brought no comfort. No one now believed in a good God given all the wretchedness that they beheld, and all discipline was thrown to the winds. Whether Imperial, Swedish or Danish – they hurried after the riders, loaded their muskets and cried: Lord, shoot me one! And shoot me two! And straightway they robbed their victims, who were still twitching with lead in their bodies, to extract a tribute from them: belts, shoes, mouldy bread. If the other side was once again victorious, Bavarians or Poles without flag or territory, things did not go well for them either, oh no. The trees hung full with the strangest of fruits.

Naked and beaten, we stayed behind, shivering by the remains of the ovens, and carried away with everything was the hope that man was not merely beast to man, that he could also be a comfort to him. Some spoke of a curse that lay upon the place, poisonous whispering filled the alleyways, witches' talk: Why does my neighbour still have a fur, a sack of corn? By what misdeed does he have his wine, by what betrayal? Why do hares run into this one's trap, why do fishes bite for that one even without a worm? And always fog crept over the lake, even on sunny days, and the eyes of people mute with fear and hunger saw new dread in it, the next fresh breath of hell.

For a long time the author of these lines, sitting at his table wrapped in nettle-cloth, could not see whence ease-fulness would come. Black with fat crows, mutely consuming what lay upon the fields of slaughter, the tips of the trees loomed from the mist, and the tip of the prayer-house, the little gabled tower with the cross, were just visible. A good man, the cooper Milger, had tarred the roof and half-timbering at his own expense, and as the mist roiled it looked as if the chapel was floating lightly over the water.

Behind the window, the bullseye glass, a tiny light lit by a pious traveller burned. A bell sounded faintly, and suddenly the old scribe felt as if he could see more than just a tallow candle, even after he had rubbed his eyes: as if the pain of tormented souls glowed there to show him the way. And fired by the joy of knowing what it was that could bring healing to us and to the one who had gone ahead, he rose cheering from his chair and accidentally knocked the earthen vessel in which he dipped his pen. Whereupon, oh!, the ink spilled over his bread and cheese.

The cock, whose comb had been bitten off in the night by a fox or marten that had broken into the coop, had stopped crowing. But since the attack on the school Luisa was often already awake when the ticking of the metal alarm clock changed slightly, sounding brighter in the cool of morning, as if its cogs were suddenly made of glass. The sun was still hidden behind the stables, and the breath of the ravens could be seen when they jumped from one furrow to another to pick something from the earth. People in grey work clothes and caps marched along the forest rim near Kluvensiek, a long row of them. Most had spades, shovels or picks over their shoulders, and some pulled a cart full of uniformed men. With carbines on their backs, they let their legs dangle and smoked, and once she thought she heard them laughing. But perhaps it was the croaking of the ravens.

She slipped quickly into her coat and took the milk jug from the table. The long laces of her boots were still untied, and Motte, his shaggy hair full of nettles, panted along beside her as they crossed the courtyard, and snapped at them. A wood-burning lorry rattled slowly along the road towards the convent; painted on the driver's door were the words: 'Görres Potato Wholesaler', but on the bed of the lorry were new coffins smelling of sawdust, stacked higher than the driver's cabin. Only a few people were waiting outside the dairy. This morning the milk was being poured out not by Herr Thamling but by the milker who had been standing in the door in the roof a few days before, in his vest. Now he was wearing an almost new pullover with a zip, and the thighs and seat of his blue canvas trousers were so thickly smeared with old milk fat that they looked as if they were made of leather. 'Well look here, if it isn't the little sister of the sun that lights up the farmyard . . .' he said, a match between his lips. 'Give me that jug!'

He had slightly sunken cheeks and clear green eyes that looked brown in the shadow, and was about the same age as most of the workers or apprentices who had not been seconded from this strategically important activity: seventeen or eighteen. His facial expression was like that of his colleagues at this time of day: once the hard and often hectic morning's work had been accomplished and the hearty breakfast eaten in Frau Thamling's kitchen, a peaceable vacancy and sometimes even a slight roguishness appeared on their features, the shimmer of an easier life.

But unlike the ones who always gave off a smell of old sweat, of herbal cigarettes and last night's spirits, he smelled of soap, with a note of lavender. His dark blond hair, carefully combed back from his forehead, had a slight sheen, his chin was clean-shaven, and his fingernails weren't rimmed with dirt, or at least they weren't as tarry as the fingernails of the others.

'You're Luisa, isn't that right?'

She smiled and nodded; she liked his voice. It sounded older than he looked, and both as strong and as gentle as it needed to be for someone who worked with animals every day. After he had filled her jug, she asked him for some quark, of which her father was so fond, and he took a spatula, drew the parchment paper from the vat and said, 'By the way, from my attic room I can see into yours, one little corner. All those books . . . Why do you read so much? And such great doorstoppers too. Do girls your age have nothing better to do?'

The milk in the tiled basin on the floor behind him looked velvety, and she pulled a face, only slightly so as not to insult him. 'Why?' she asked. 'What should they do instead?'

'Well, I don't know,' he replied. 'Giggle, perhaps? Stroke rabbits? Or bake a chocolate cake that tastes like charcoal?'

That made her laugh, and he twisted the lid of her jug open and skimmed the quark into the cavity. Then he looked past her at the fighter planes on the horizon, a small relay, and said: 'Billie also told me about your favourite, the grey one that had its ear shot off . . .' He ran his finger over a tiny nick on his chin. 'I know you mean well, girl, but milk and bits of butter give us strength – they're not meant for horses, certainly not when their hooves are diseased. Too much protein only makes things even worse, and in the end they can't even limp to the knacker's yard.'

Without paying any heed to the waiting people, who were stamping querulously on the spot in the morning chill, he studied her for a few moments and continued in a quieter voice: 'I've put a bag of bran in the corridor for you. There are nettles and camomile blossoms mixed in with it. One scoop twice a day, with a lot of water. Add some good hay, you'll find that above the byre, but don't get caught . . . And if you've got some aspirins at home, you can happily crumble those in too. And then make sure that the mare is always standing on something nice and soft, ideally sawdust, slightly moistened. So far only the hooves are inflamed, and she might rally, you never know.'

When he whispered his voice sounded hoarse, which made the hairs on Luisa's arms stir as if an insect was moving over them. She was so amazed that she didn't know what to say, she just stared at him, and he continued in a normal voice: 'My name is Walter, by the way, but you can call me Ata, everybody else does. Probably because my best friend is called Imi.' He winked at her. 'At the weekend there's free beer and music at the Fährhof, are you coming along? I've always wanted to swing a chestnut filly around the place.'

His teeth were even in a way that you only normally saw in pictures outside the cinema or in photographs in magazines, and Luisa, who took his smile for confirmation of his invitation, felt suddenly breathless. 'Really? But I'm not allowed to go to a pub,' she replied and thought immediately of her sister's midnight-blue dress, which she could borrow and alter. 'At least not without my parents. And I actually have to go to bed at nine.'

He shook his head and spat out the match on the floor. 'Really? That's a shame. They'll still be tuning their instruments by then . . .' he said, apparently saddened, then filled an old man's jug and wrapped him a piece of butter. 'But all right, I'll wait for a while. Patience is a sign of affection, or whatever it is that they say. See you!'

The sun shone through the stained-glass window onto the full basins, and with a quiet grunt Luisa tapped her temple and left. But she hadn't reached the first step of the ramp before she looked back from the corner of her eyes, slightly disappointed that he hadn't pressed the point, hadn't persisted with his invitation beyond kidding around. He hummed to himself as he worked, and with each step that she took away from him the sweeter was the strange tugging feeling beneath her breastbone, as if she had just swallowed a spoonful of the palest honey.

*

She spent the morning putting Frau Mangoldt's books on the shelf. She wrote the titles down in her notebook, and her sister kept coming into the room to ask her the where-abouts of various clothes or shoes. The garret room smelled of her hair in the curling iron and the turpentine with which she rubbed the old polish from her nails.

'Why are you making such a fuss?' asked Luisa. 'It's just a lunch. Or are you trying to outdo Gudrun?'

Sirens in Sehestedt, and the sound of the canal ferry could only just be heard in the smoke belched out by the fog machine. 'What do I want? To outdo her, a drop of cherry juice on my lips would be enough,' Billie said. 'She'll be wearing her classroom bun again, and her hand-knitted jacket, want to bet? You could put her in the gunners' trench and those starving soldiers wouldn't so much as look at her arse!'

Luisa snorted over a book. 'And why should they if they're hungry,' she said. 'And I don't think her jacket's too bad. The knitting pattern's called "Meander". It's nice and long, and I'm sure it keeps her snug and warm.'

'Yes, and nice and grey, you forgot to say. She looks like a ball of wool in that thing. Always keep your backside good and flat and don't show your waist, it might arouse desires! And then she's surprised that nobody's got her in the family way by the age of thirty . . . And how's the dress, by the way? Papa brought it. Too short?'

Luisa, kneeling on the carpet, tied a knot in a frayed ribbon bookmark before looking up. 'It fits quite well, but the bodice is too tight,' she said, 'you can see between the buttons. And constantly picking on Gudrun won't make you any better. Just be a bit kinder. The fact that we're living in this flat rather than some sort of stable or Nissen hut like the other bombed-out people is also down to her!'

Now the Eider Bridge was swathed in smoke, the smell of sulphur came in through the draughty windows, and Billie put a foot on the chair and straightened her stocking. 'Is that right? Well, if you say so . . . Take a look, real Perlon, by Kunert in the Sudetenland. They've actually switched entirely to military production: parachute silk, thread for surgeons and so on. But of course there are still special places for special gentlemen. They're exquisite, like silk.'

Luisa didn't look up and went on flicking through a book full of pictures of plants, and her sister came closer.

'Incidentally, a bodice can't be too tight, bear that in mind. And always a few dabs of red somewhere and the right perfume, that'll open hearts to you. Or the wallets that are worn over the hearts.' She considered the shelf and frowned: 'What are you doing there, you crazy little thing? What's that going to be when it's finished? Lewis Carroll and Erich Kästner at the top left and Hans Christian Andersen in the middle? And why does Margaret Mitchell come before Karl May? Do you want me to write out the alphabet for you?'

Luisa pushed her away. 'Thanks, I'd rather not; your handwriting looks like weeds.' She pulled her pencil out from behind her ear and tapped the volumes. 'Here, *Alice in Wonderland* is of course the first book, before *Emil and the Detectives*, *Fairy Tales* and *Gone with the Wind*. And *Winnetou* comes after *Nutcracker and Mouse King*. That's about as alphabetical as it gets, isn't it?'

With her eyes wide with disbelief, her sister turned up her collar. 'But who does it that way!' she exclaimed, with a crystal button between her teeth. 'Have you never been to the library? Or a bookshop? You act so bookish at twelve years old, and don't know that you arrange old tomes by author?'

Luisa turned away to hide her embarrassment, her fluttering eyelids. By the time she started school the bookshop had been burned out, and she had always ordered her reading matter from Beuker's the stationers. 'I don't care, I won't bother,' she insisted. 'I don't want anybody finding anything, least of all you; there are no fashion magazines.

And take some Odol: Vinzent's going to be out of the door backwards when he smells your onion breath.'

When they went down to the Thamlings' – the sound of planes was in the air again – Sibylle was wearing a sleeveless red dress with ruching at the neckline and gold hoop earrings. Her mother, the hairline above her forehead blackened with charred cork, had put on her uniform jacket and skirt from her time with Winter Relief, and she groaned with each step she took because her orthopaedic shoes pinched. Luisa looked through the corridor window into the open barn. 'Gudrun's there already!' she said. 'I think they've got a new car!'

Black as the tarred plinths of the pillars it stood in the shadow of the tractor, and would have been almost invisible without the white tyre walls and chrome bumpers. It was a big Horch with a winged arrow emblem, and her father straightened his tie and murmured: 'Bloody hell, what a battleship. Straight out of Göring's garage!' With a hiss his wife motioned him to be quiet, and then the mezzanine door opened; Sophia Thamling smiled at them. A delicate woman with white hair and a face filled with kindness, her voice was now a whisper; during the attack by low-flying planes a few months earlier she had been wounded in the neck by some shrapnel. She smoothed her white apron before shaking hands with each of them, and even giving Luisa a kiss on the cheek. 'I've nearly finished it!' she muttered close to her ear. Her eyes were light blue, almost aquamarine. 'Does he get away?'

The girl raised a finger to her lips, and the woman disappeared into the kitchen with a smile. The smell of broth and fried poultry filled the hall of the grand apartment, which was well heated as always; there were big tiled stoves. The one in the dining room even had a brass chandelier, and the ceiling was decorated with frescoes: putti, birds and the goddess Demeter, a cornucopia of fruits pouring into the blue sky. The wine glasses on the oval table glittered, and Gudrun, who was waiting in an armchair next to the sideboard and flicking through a magazine, raised her head and cried, 'Heavens, Mama, what's up with your shoes? They're far too tight! Have you got swollen ankles again?'

She stood up quickly and her mother nodded anxiously and hugged her eldest daughter, uttering a quivering groan. 'Oh, my child, I miss you! No one is as perceptive as you!' she said, making her voice sound weaker than it was. 'Couldn't you make some of that chestnut ointment for me again? It did me a lot of good and was always absorbed immediately. My stockings never got greasy.'

Gudrun dabbed some soot from her forehead with the tip of her thumb. 'But of course, Mummy dearest! I'll see to it that you get some tomorrow,' she said. She hugged her stepfather too and extended a hand to Luisa. She shook her head briefly as she did so, a hint of disapproval less for her black polo-neck pullover than the greenish-brown men's trousers, comfortable tweed which had worn out at the knees. Gudrun was even a Führerin in the district women's association.

Her skirt was pleated, and as expected she was wearing the same knitted jacket with the staghorn buttons. Only her hairnet was new: tiny pearls shimmered on her bun. She also shook hands with Billie, as if she hadn't noticed her beady appraisal; she went to the sideboard and filled a few sparkling wine glasses with Bernkasteler. 'Vine-leaf extract pills are also supposed to be good for tired legs. They're hard to get hold of right now, but I'll have the pharmacist get some up from his bunker.'

She distributed the glasses, and Luisa's father, who had stirred into his quark not only some bottled cherries but also a slug of cognac, slumped onto the nearest chair. 'You get blonder and blonder, is that possible? Suits me, having a stepdaughter like that. And where have the administrator and his district secretary got to?' He lit a cigarette and looked towards the hatch, from beyond which Silesian dialect could be heard: the kitchen maids. 'Hey, Sophia, where's Klaas? Aren't you going to come and raise a glass?'

Gudrun smiled indulgently, slid a silver ashtray towards him and said, 'They're on their way, Dad, they've just got to get their work out of the way. We're going to need all kinds of extra help next week because they're calling up the last men, and the army supply office is applying a fair amount of pressure. Those pen-pushers know nothing at all about farming, now they're even telling us to slaughter our heifers. But I can tell you this: today is a very special day, there's something to celebrate. Cheers, then!'

Luisa had been given a sip of sparkling wine as well, and Billie winked at her. 'Oh, that's why!' she said, brushed a curl behind her ear and dabbed at the creole earring with the serpentine chasing. 'I was wondering why you'd smartened yourself up so much. A warm charcoal suit always works, doesn't it? And the hairnet and those stockings! A hint of sin. Are they from Kunert in the Sudetengau?'

Gudrun looked down at herself. 'What? Why?' she asked, baffled. 'No idea, I was given them by . . .' She waved a hand. 'The things you notice, sis, it's typical of you. But we really shouldn't be dwelling on things like that these days, should we? Couldn't the Jungvolk or the BDM teach you what our true gems are? The men are fighting for us to the bitter end, the borders are ablaze, and there may well be more important things in a German woman's life than make-up and fine clothes.'

'Really?' Billie asked, with the glass to her smiling mouth. The smooth rim was red with her lipstick, and there seemed to be a sparkle in her voice. 'And what might those be?'

Her half-sister, who wore the triangular insignia on her jacket, the life-rune, looked at her from top to toe and seemed to be about to reply; but at that moment Vinzent and the administrator came into the room, both rubbing their hands. They were followed by a gust of February air, and the irritation in Gudrun's eyes faded after a flutter of her lashes. She set down her glass, tapped the gong on the sideboard with her knuckle and called: 'Sophia? Are you ready? We can go!'

*

The sun pierced the clouds and shone through the high windows with the velvet curtains, and the thickly painted flowers and apples below the ceiling cast patches of pale pink on the tablecloth. Because Luisa was sitting right next to the double door, Vinzent greeted her first. His head, dark-haired, was angular, the back of his neck shaved high, like the area above his ears, where the stubble already had a silvery glint; his fortieth birthday was imminent. Thick brows like little brushes shaded his eyes, and he jutted his chin further forward than natural and said, 'Well, sister-in-law? Not only are you smart, you're getting prettier by the day. Where will it end?'

He discreetly tickled the palm of her hand with his thumb, and Luisa's smile was not entirely one of thanks for the compliment. In fact, given his double-breasted suit with its sharp creases and rectangular padded shoulders she couldn't help thinking of her father's words: 'He's stitched roof trusses into them!' The blue silk tie and the pocket handkerchief had a pattern of tiny lilies and his shoes were also two-tone, dark blue and white. 'Riga,' he said, when he noticed the way she was looking. 'Those Jews know a thing or two about shoe-making.'

Herr Thamling also wore a suit, his crumpled black one with the embroidered waistcoat, although of course she knew that there wasn't a watch on the end of the gold chain, but a cigarette lighter. He emanated a faint smell of the stable, and his white hair was thin and translucent in the sunlight, his moustache a dull yellow from smoking. He slumped in his chair at the end of the table, looked at Luisa and said, 'Your window was dark last night. Finished all your books? There's still a stack in the basement, I can show you them tomorrow.'

She nodded, smiled with pleasure and unfolded the starched napkin: Frau Thamling brought in the soup, a big tureen of beef broth with marrow balls and strips of pancake. In a pot-bellied carafe in front of her there was bright gold elderflower cordial, Luisa's favourite drink, with bits of ice and mint leaves floating in it. The others were drinking French red wine, a pre-war Bordeaux, and they clinked glasses and wished each other a pleasant meal.

A one-armed woman, also in a white apron, brought another little bowl of freshly chopped cabbage in from the kitchen, and the empty sleeve of her blouse, which she simply allowed to dangle, brushed Luisa's cheek. 'Well?' her father asked, already visibly heated after only a few spoonfuls: his forehead had reddened. 'What sort of surprise is this? Are they about to unleash the miracle weapon? Or is Vinzent finally about to be appointed secretary of state for agriculture and forestry, or whatever it's called?'

Vinzent dabbed his mouth with his napkin and said, 'Heaven preserve us, Willi! Let's just be happy that we have the current one, he's saved us from a number of unreasonable demands on the part of Berlin. Some people's wisdom stops at the edge of their desk; they think a war is won from one day to the next.' He looked at his wife with a grin. 'But we have a kind of miracle of our own to announce, don't we? A gift from heaven. But one thing at a time . . .'

He reached into the basket and buttered a piece of the warm bread, pressing the knife down so hard that the butter appeared in the holes on the other side. 'So, yesterday we were at Hinrich's . . .'

Gudrun passed him the salt. 'Lohse, he means, our Gauleiter.'

Vinzent smacked his lips. 'Exactly, him. He was cele-
brating his twentieth anniversary, which deserved a drop.
And of course we didn't just talk about the requisitions, we
also talked about this farm. General van Cleef, the owner,
has fallen and sadly there is no longer any doubt, and there
are no heirs either. At any rate not in the Reich. And as
Hinrich always says: uncertainty in matters of property
spoils the harvest. For which reason I have . . .' He shook
his head and took a deep breath. 'I have responded to his
urgent request, further reinforced by the Reich Food
Authority and the topmost leadership, and on the basis of
my experiences in local matters not entirely excessive, and
put myself forward as owner of this estate.'

Wheezing, he smoothed the napkin tucked into his
waistcoat and the general silence, underlined by the occasional frown, was filled with reflection on his odd phrasing.
But Gudrun beamed, raised her glass and looked encour-
agingly around at the party. 'What do you think, isn't that
fabulous?' she exclaimed. 'Isn't it entirely marvellous? One
thousand nine hundred hectares plus forest, for a symbolic
price!'

Her husband stifled a cough, as if a crumb had stuck in
his throat. 'Well, yes,' he said quickly, 'that's probably what
they call it. But of course the duties to the staff and to eco-
nomic viability are more than symbolic. I will not only
receive such profits as there may be – I will also have to
deal with the torrent of losses that are being suffered these
days. And God knows the property tax isn't exactly going
to be a piece of cake either. But let's not think about that

now.' He too raised his glass. 'Cheers, then, my dear ones! Good luck!'

They congratulated him and took a sip, and Billie, who had pushed her plate aside after only a few morsels, linked her fingers behind her neck and revealed the red hairs in her armpit. 'Well heavens above! Doesn't take long to become a landowner these days, does it?' she said. 'I think I'll have to get myself a Party membership card.' The old chair creaked as she swayed her hips with a giggle. 'Will you be living here in the manor house as well?'

Gudrun took a breath, but Vinzent answered:

'Rubbish, it has nothing to do with a membership card, and everything to do with the desire to assume responsibility! And for now we'll be staying at the Krähenberg, it's splendid enough for us there. The bunker has just been reinforced, with modernized ventilation and new steel doors. Gas-proof! And besides, we're so fond of the canal view.'

Luisa could still feel the touch of the woman's sleeve on her cheek, and nervously ran her hand over it. Her father, whose lower lip was already dark rimmed, reached behind him and took a new bottle of Bordeaux from the side table. 'And what else?' he asked as he turned the corkscrew. 'Was that the miracle? Or what did you mean by "one thing at a time"?'

Vinzent put an arm around his wife's shoulders. With a vague smile he raised his chin and his eyes turned curiously round, as if something ominous were happening behind her. 'Right, Willi, there is one more small thing that we don't want to conceal from you,' he replied and ran the tip of his tongue over his lips. 'We weren't able to come out with it straight away, it had to stay a secret for a while, because we already had various . . . well anyway. But now we have certainty, and you too will see it soon.' He gave a little cough. 'How should I put it . . . Due obeisance is being done to the dynastic imperative, the succession is secured: my dear wife is pregnant!'

The administrator clapped his hands. 'Well, bravo!' he said. 'And not before time. I urgently need a tractor driver.'

Almost everyone laughed, and Vinzent drew his wife to him and grinned at everyone with ironic pride, although he closed his eyelids at the sight of Sibylle's expression, one of sudden alarm. Her mother raised both hands to her mouth. 'Oh good God in heaven, is that really true?' she murmured and her eyes filled with tears. 'Has the Holy Virgin heard my years of prayer? So you are fertile, my child? I mean you are with child?'

Gudrun blanched. Her shy, strangely sorrowful smile vanished and she looked past her out of the window and said under her breath, almost without moving her lips, 'Since when have you prayed, Mama? You've never stepped inside a church, not even for your wedding. And if you want to know precisely: I have often had cause for joy, albeit only briefly . . . But now I'm in my fourth month.'

Her mother bit her lip and moaned ecstatically – it sounded almost like a whimper – Luisa's father topped up the wine glasses, and now everyone was congratulating her, even Sibylle, although she didn't shake her hand. She just raised her glass, smiled with one corner of her mouth and set it down again without drinking. And already the colour was returning to Gudrun's features, the light to her eyes, and she nudged her husband with her elbow. 'About church,' she said. 'You must tell me who our little boy's godfather will be!'

Vinzent shook his head gently and ate some more broth. 'Come now, my dear, with all due understanding of your good fortune: let's wait a little for that one,' he replied. 'He told me in passing on the telephone, but even he can't predict the course of events. Who knows how things will be in five months' time.'

Gudrun who had formed a silent 'Admiral Dönitz!' with her lips for everyone, raised her blonde eyebrows. 'Why? What's going to happen?' she said, startled. 'People die, people come into the world and are baptized, whether today or who knows when. And after the final victory we will go back to Kiel, order a ceremony from Pastor Schimmel and have a big party, as we should!'

Her mother nodded with agreement, but Billie grunted into her glass. 'After the what?' she murmured, and ignored her father as he cleared his throat. 'You're dreaming, my little flower. Lift your eyes from your crochet-work for war widows and look out of the window. The British have been laughing in the face of our anti-aircraft fire, and are massing in broad daylight. Here, our little one almost died at school the other day. And your Kiel, the one you want to go back to, is just a heap of rubble thanks to your Führer, or so we hear; you could have your "little boy" baptized with dust.'

The ice in Luisa's carafe crackled softly and Gudrun made a face as if the sun were shining in her eyes. 'I'm sorry? What sort of tone is that?' She turned towards her husband and wiped some parsley from his tie. 'Did she just call me an idiot? Is it possible that my sister is becoming a little arrogant?'

Vinzent ran his finger along the rim of his glass, a fine gold line, and murmured: 'That's enough, now, let's stay calm. Perhaps we should . . .'

'Stepsister!' Billie interrupted, still not taking her eyes off Gudrun. 'Does that mean you're deaf too? Everyone has a radio, everyone knows it's over, don't they? That the Americans will soon be crossing the Rhine, the Russians are at the gates of Berlin and the miracle weapon is just so much nonsense. Every soldier who is still being sent into the field is dying for nothing whatsoever, and the sooner they chase your Hitler and his riffraff all the way to hell, the better for us!'

For a moment everyone seemed to freeze; spoons hovered over plates. Her father shook his head disapprovingly, and her mother folded her napkin together and then unfolded it again and looked anxiously around. 'Yes, why is it always "your" Hitler?' she said. 'He's your Hitler too, darling, you owe him a lot! Just think of the rhythmic gymnastics and the pretty neckerchief with the leather woggle they gave you at the BDM. And now please leave your wine be, you've hardly eaten anything!'

'Oh really?' Sibylle drank anyway, some of the liquid trickling out of the corner of her mouth. 'And where did my Führer lead me to? Without him and his endless war my school wouldn't have closed and I'd have graduated long ago and could study in Berlin or Munich,' she went on. 'Maybe even in Paris. Instead I'm rotting away on this godforsaken farm and getting bored senseless in that draughty shack up there, where it never gets really warm and I get one case of cystitis after another.'

Frau Thamling straightened her black velvet choker. 'But dear child! You can come down here and sit by the stove any time you like,' she said hoarsely. 'Your little sister does that too. I make tea from raspberry leaves, bake raisin buns, and we chat and read . . .'

'Or you could come to mine,' the administrator said and looked at his watch. 'I've got more than enough work to keep you warm. The firewood needs fetching from the forest, the slurry needs to go on the fields, and I'll soon need all hands in the byre. Otherwise you could look after wounded men in the convent. The nuns would welcome you with open arms.'

He grinned at her with a wink, and Billie pulled a face at him. Her arms folded under her breasts, her chin raised, she stared out of the window with moist eyelids at the empty courtyard, and for the first time Luisa noticed that there were lighter amber-coloured facets in her dark brown eyes.

'But perhaps . . .' Gudrun said and made a mouth as though she was sucking something sweet, '. . . perhaps you have cystitis for quite other reasons? Is that possible? One hears things.'

Then Vinzent struck the table with the palm of his hand; the cutlery clattered, the salt jumped out of the little bowl. 'That'll do, that's quite enough!' he repeated, and 'enough' acquired a menacing weight. He pushed his empty glass away. 'We are amongst friends here, I mean we are family, and I am convinced that no one here listens to the foreign broadcaster, that stupid propaganda. And yet: even under my roof it's better for us to think before we speak, Sibylle. We have something to celebrate, damn it all, so keep your poison to yourself!'

Frau Thamling carefully collected the soup bowls, steaming plates were brought from the kitchen, and for a moment Vinzent himself seemed surprised by the silence that followed his admonition. He gripped the end of his shirt collar with two fingers as if to stretch it, and pulled back his sleeves to reveal cufflinks bearing the coat of arms of his office, the sword and the ear of corn. Gudrun scooped potatoes onto his plate.

Wind whirled dust over the yard and made the cable ring rattle against the empty flagpole, and while he was chopping the potatoes into little pieces he didn't seem to notice Billie glaring at him across the table. Her eyes shaded by her eyebrows, she gnawed at the inside of her lip as if biting back the curses and maledictions that she would so have liked to utter, and the tips of her fingernails left fine red lines on the white cambric. His wife pushed the gravy boat towards him. 'You were about to address the question of accommodation, by the way,' she said gently. 'Shouldn't we do that straight away? Darling?'

He cleared his throat and took a sip of water. 'Correct,' he said, looking around. 'The accommodation . . . We need to look at that as well. Of course we are still ready to help, because we still have room, at least in the barns and stables. But there really isn't much sense in our putting the officers' families up here in the house. That could make people reach false conclusions. I mean, if someone were ever actually to . . .'

Luisa's mother clapped her hands together. 'Oh, my God, Vinzent!' she cut in. 'What a far-sighted son-in-law you are! Those are my very own thoughts, my words, quite precisely! Recently I told him right here: the Russkies will twist our intentions if we take them in. If they get a single whiff of the SS . . .'

Her husband rested his fingertips on her arm, but she batted them away. 'I said, let me finish! Of course the Russkies will see red and think we're all the same. They will burn the place down around our ears over a few runes and send us all to Siberia. Or they will hang us all from the linden tree in the yard, even without medals and Party membership cards!'

Although Vinzent was smiling politely, his cheekbones were twitching. 'No, no, you've misunderstood me now,' he said. 'Apart from the fact that I myself am in the association, Gerda: I thought, here under this roof things are really a bit rudimentary, we can agree with Billie on that, can't we? Nothing but papered boards over the roof tiles, a makeshift kitchen, a mildewed bathroom . . .' He turned towards the administrator. 'And I've been wondering whether we shouldn't do up the villa of that Jewish professor, Klaas. He won't be coming back anyway and it's bound to be more spacious and comfortable. Not that the Gauleiter's really going to look in and think we're neglecting his protégées. Still, they are the wives of standard-bearers!'

Herr Thamling nodded and made a note, and as Gudrun

poured her husband some water she gave her mother a reproachful look. 'Or something . . .' she said, and dipped her nose into her red-wine glass.

At that moment the meat was brought in, crisply roasted pieces of turkey surrounded by all kinds of green vegetables and marinated mushrooms on a silver platter, and amidst the general 'Ahs!' and 'Ohs!' no one noticed at first that Sibylle was getting up from the table. It was only when she threw the napkin with the lipstick stains onto her empty plate and got up that the others looked at her and noticed the running mascara under her eyes. But no one said anything, bowls full of peas and carrots were passed around, wine and water topped up, and she sniffled as she left the room.

During the meal, the chat about preferences for breast or thigh meat and laughter about the fluting notes that Luisa's father produced from a bone, she could be heard pacing back and forth under the roof. Her heels hammered on the floorboards, the teardrops on the chandelier quivered under her footsteps, and Frau Thamling looked up with a frown at the frescoes, the angels and roses against the cerulean blue. Gudrun rested a hand on her husband's. 'I think,' she said, chewing, 'we should give my sister a pair of slippers.'

*

In the stable Breeze was waiting close by the gate, her uninjured ear turned towards Luisa. Her mane and her light-coloured coat were already less scruffy than they had been a few days before, and her eyes were a bit brighter. To make standing less painful, the horse alternately lifted one leg and then the other onto a hoof-tip, and Luisa scooped some of the bran mixed with grass into the fodder stone and crumbled two aspirins over it. The animal snorted, and as it ate she groomed it carefully with a soft body-brush and giggled when its thin tail flicked into her face.

That morning the milk was being distributed by the refugee woman who had issued the advice about scratching her mouth when the Russians came. She was wearing an old fur and a Wehrmacht cap and she poured a litre into her jug, and when Luisa waited for a second one the old woman shook her head and said, 'That's all there is, child. It got requisitioned last night seeing as how they need strength for their war. God alive, the people are hungry and cold and they couldn't give a damn about the father-land and all that nonsense as long as they could go on living in Bunzel or Gruttke and eating poppyseed buns. Now if you could kindly step aside . . .'

Swinging her unusually light jug Luisa walked across the courtyard to the byre. The huge room held over three hundred animals, and once again there were almost only women working here now, scraping the dung together, filling the racks with hay or rinsing out the tubs and buckets. The refugees from the rural east could be identified by the fact that they wore their headscarves as triangles over their hair and tied under their chins, while the women from the cities, the bombed-out ones, mostly wore them as turbans, with the knot over their foreheads. One of them was even milking with painted nails.

Walter was leaning against one of the boxes for pregnant

cattle, and winked at her. 'This could be tough.' He was wearing blue overalls and had a bit of stubble on his chin, which Luisa liked, and she set down her jug and joined him in looking over the chest-high wall. 'Yes, it looks like damned hard work,' he confirmed. 'Would you mind giving me a hand?'

Sun shone through the stable window on the fresh straw. The cow, almost entirely brown – with only a white blaze – seemed to be young, and wasn't chained. Its big eyes dull and unseeing, it paced slowly around in the spacious shed, its full udder swaying and the tips of its horns sometimes brushing the walls. There were grooves in the whitewash, a wavy line made by the many cows that had come before it. The amniotic sac was already protruding beneath the root of the cow's tail, darkly transparent in the light; some dark fur and a hoof could be seen in the pink water, and Luisa asked: 'Already? Isn't it far too early? I thought the new calves came in May?'

Walter took off his watch and put it in his ruler pocket. 'Normally,' he said and opened the metal door. 'But what does that mean today? Even the animals are aware of the war. Many go sterile because they don't want to bring anything else into the world, others retain their fat and give thinner milk, and the pregnant ones miscarry; that's in the Bible. Well, and here we have not only a heifer who is doing all this for the first time, but also a breach birth as you can tell by the hooves, a right mess . . .' He held the animal firmly by the horn, placed a listening ear to its hip joint and pointed to the open door beside the box, the equipment room. 'Fetch me the medical case.'

By this he meant a rusty bucket hanging on the wall among rubber aprons. It contained screw clamps and forceps with wooden jaws, and scalpels, scissors and bent needles gleamed in a jar with a lid. Luisa knew similar instruments from the hospital where she had once had to have stitches in her knee, and the black thread on the roll looked more like a fishing reel. Walter cut a section of it off.

Then he clapped the animal on the neck and kicked gently against the tarsal bone, again and again, until it sank down on its front knees. The animal's back legs remained upright, and he reached for the dung-encrusted tassel, bent back the tail and tied it to a horn. 'The milk-harp,' he said with a grin, and sure enough as soon as he plucked the cord stretched tightly over the cow's body a soft bass note sounded. 'It'll kick off in a minute.'

Luisa was instructed to push more straw behind the snorting creature, a thick layer, and she took off her scarf, slipped from her coat and had just scattered the second armful and knocked it into shape when the sac tore. The amniotic fluid, a warm torrent, poured over her hands, and her skirt and woollen stockings became wet as well. Startled, she pulled a face and looked at Walter. But he laughed. 'What's wrong, it's good for you!' he said. 'It contains all the good things you need to live if you happen to be a cow. But unfortunately no printed letters . . .'

The fluid smelled like the scent that rises from freshly slaughtered animals, and he felt the still soft, cream-coloured hooves of the calf, and ran his thumbnail through the trickles. Then he pulled carefully on the fetlocks, and the mother closed her eyes, stretched her neck and mooed loudly: tethered by the hay-racks, the other cows interrupted their ruminating and turned their heads. Walter scratched the back of his neck. 'The product doesn't come all by itself,' he murmured, and fetched a spade from the tool-room.

He twined two ropes, finger-thick and stiff with old blood, around the cannon bone of the calf, whose black shiny nostrils, pink inside, were already visible. Then he knotted the ends around the wooden handle, grabbed it with both fists, took two steps back and adopted a position with his legs apart on the gleaming straw. 'No, no,' he said when Luisa squatted down and stroked the cow's neck, whispering comforting words. 'Please keep away. She has to come to terms with it by herself, that's just how life is from now on. If she lashes out with her head from the pain, you'll get a horn in your belly.'

The girl stepped aside but didn't take her eyes off the panting animal. Its wet eyelids were closed, dust and wheat-husks stuck to them, and as they waited in silence for the next contraction they heard planes, further away than they had been in the previous few days, and a burst of machine-gun fire somewhere by the canal. The animal emitted some disgusting farts and called out again, a deep dark sound at first but one which became shriller with each beat of its heavy heart, until Luisa held her hands to her ears.

Gritting his teeth, the knuckles of his fist white, Walter pulled with all his strength on the handle, the taut cords, and watery blood poured from the vulva. Now the whole head of the calf appeared, the shiny black neck, covered with scraps of mucous membrane: as if it had no neck bones its head dangled between the stiff legs, the tips of its ears brushing the straw. And suddenly the umbilical broke, the contraction ebbed away and Walter blew out his cheeks.

The pelvis and the hindquarters were still inside the mother animal, and he shook his head and said: 'A bull calf, that's typical. First they're the wrong way round then they're too stupid to find the teats, and in the end they mount the tractor in the field. Come here, girl, take over from me!'

Luisa, gnawing on her lip, dragged herself away from the sight of the new-born calf whose pale tongue hung from its mouth, slipped under Walter's arms and reached for the handle. 'Exactly right,' he said. His hands were raw, his breath tickled the back of her neck. 'I knew you were a natural midwife. Keep the ropes taut or else this will go on for ever. Press your pelvis down, brace your heels on the floor and take a deep breath. Ready?'

She said yes, and a jerk ran through her armpits as soon as he left her to bear the weight. The tug on her limbs was familiar from sailing on the Förde or flying kites in the autumn; after only a few moments her arms began to tremble. She made herself hard and pressed her lips together, and Walter blew into the calf's nostrils and reached into its mouth to remove the mucus. Then he opened a junction box on the wall, took out a stone bottle and took a swig before pouring some of the spirits over the animal's body, on the bloody area around the navel. As he did so he whistled a tune.

Luisa broke into a sweat and she groaned faintly,

although Walter didn't seem to hear her. As he picked scraps of the amniotic sac off the calf, gently massaged its heart region and ran an exploratory hand over the mother animal's belly, Luisa's feet started slipping on the smooth straw, and she got cramp in her calves. She bared her teeth, bent back with all her strength, and when the effort was so great that a fart escaped her, which made her almost die of shame, he just shook his head and said, 'The parquet floor creaks horribly here . . . Just keep up the tension!'

Sweat ran into her eyes, and her knees and thighs were trembling now as well. 'But I can't!' she cried and closed her stinging lids tightly. 'Please, help me! It's slipping back!'

Walter drank some more schnapps and calmly corked the bottle. 'Of course it's slipping back,' he said. 'It doesn't want to come into this world, you can understand that, can't you? Particularly since it's coming far too early . . . But you still have to keep the cords taut. Given the position of the animal's back it mustn't kink or you may as well call the slaughterman right away.' He closed the junction box. 'Now pull yourself together, Madam Professor! Anyone who can lug such heavy books around every day isn't going to let a calf drag her back into the cow!'

New shudders ran through its fur, dung dripped on its hooves. A broad ray of sunshine duplicated the shadows of its horns, and it opened its red-rimmed eyes wide and stretched its neck again, but seemed too weak to roar. It managed only a hoarse panting sound, almost a groan, laid its ears back and raised its rump: and now the rest of the new-born came, pelvis and hindquarters all came into the light with a smacking sound. Luisa staggered back with surprise, tripped over a milking stool and fell onto the straw at almost the same time as the calf.

Even though the straw was damp and bloody and the stalks scratched the back of her neck, she lay there for a moment gasping for breath. In the far distance a tinny bell, a fire alarm, somewhere a dog barked and quickly, as if elated, the cow got to its feet and turned round, strangely yellow milk spilling from its udder, from all its teats.

Apart from its hooves, which were now getting oddly darker, the calf was completely black, with grey tips to its horns, and its whole body shook as its mother sniffed and licked at it, more and more persistently so that it would stand up. But at first it just slipped slackly around on the straw, shook its wet ears and emitted a reluctant snort, even a first roar that sounded like a whinny.

Walter, with his right sleeve rolled up, had stopped behind the cow. He slipped the flat of his hand between the labia, turned it around and plunged his arm up to the armpit in the still dilated vagina. Jiggling his arm he pulled out the massive afterbirth, knotted it with the amniotic sac into a brownish purple bag and placed it in front of the cow's nostrils. Then he took the broom and an enamelled bowl and quickly milked out some of the colostrum.

Meanwhile Luisa stared into the top of the cobwebbed beam construction, where birds fluttered and cats crept. Although her feet hurt and her shoulders ached, she felt that drag beneath her breastbone, the bright sweetness, and for a while she heard nothing but her own pulse in her ears. Walter drank some of the thick milk and offered her some as well, but she shook her head.

At last she straightened up, knocked the dust from her skirt, plucked the straw from her pullover and asked him what the calf would be called. In the sunlight his eyes were moss-green, and he drew down the corners of his mouth and washed his arms in the trough. 'No idea, girl. You can decide, you brought it into the world,' he said. 'It has to be a name, something beginning with K. That's the rule, because of the breeding sequence. But we can also give it a number.'

Gulping, slurping and grinding its teeth the cow swallowed its placenta, the blood dripped from its mouth and Luisa turned away, wrapped her scarf around her and looked as if she was thinking. But in fact she was still listening to the feeling in her chest, until there was hardly any trace of it, like a breath behind her breath. Something white and pale gold, those were the colours in which she saw it when she closed her eyes. 'Fine,' she said, 'then let's call it Karl May.'

She slipped into her coat, and Walter, who was leaning against the steel door, gnawed at his lower lip but otherwise showed no emotion. 'Why not, that sounds good,' he replied, and started cleaning his fingernails with a matchstick. 'It has a ring to it. Karl May, wasn't he that Indian chief?'

'No!' Luisa answered, already in the passageway, where she spread her arms with a smile and spun around. Her milk jug scraped along the wall. 'That was Kara Ben Nemsi.'

*

A few days later an army truck stood outside the byre. The tarpaulin was studded here and there with pine branches

76

for camouflage, and on the flat bed, on narrow benches, young men sat, some of them still boys, a dozen or more. Rucksacks and suitcases between them, metal boxes with the inscription 'Don't throw away!' and Luisa only recognized Walter, who was wearing a woollen cap and a coat, and writing something in a notebook on his knees, at her second glance. He was very pale, almost ashen, and his eyelids were reddened.

The engine started and he nodded to her. 'Where are you going?' she asked, but he only shrugged and pointed to the uniformed man with the rifle who was sitting by the loading flap. His eyes could hardly be seen beneath the rim of his helmet. 'And when will you be back?' she called into the noise of the vehicle as it pulled away, and the smoke from the exhaust scratched her throat. But he didn't seem to have heard her, he just raised a hand, and then the soldier lowered the tarpaulin.

It was clear to all by now that the Emperor and Wallenstein would not be impiously defied. The Emperor's men raged furiously, the houses, insofar as they had not been burnt to the ground, had been stripped of every last thread of clothes and linen. Still filled with fighting spirit, they had their bestial way with the tenderest of maidens as well as with old crones, they plucked out their eyes and threw them from the roof into the alley. And as for the men who were unable to pay for their lives and those of their loved ones, they slit their feet open and poured boiling lead into the flesh. It was clear who the assailants were at any time from those who were fled. Papist or Lutheran, it changed like the weather, and those who wished only to act as Christian folk and offered lodgings were robbed by their guests in the night and left beaten behind. The greatest evil of all was bubonic plague, a noxious miasma rose from putrefying horses, and in winter bears and wolves crept through the villages to rip to pieces all those who lay sick and shivering in the rubble, too weak for flight.

Meanwhile hope could not be crushed entirely. It lingered in people's hearts in spite of all the horror, just as there is room in a granite crevice where a drop of water or a seed survives from the time of our Lord. With the first sun, colour returned to weary eyes, brilliance to matted hair, a gently whispered song to chapped lips. The nights grew warmer, and the women in the town, most of them refugees who had been mistreated beyond the woods and now wanted a better life, bore bloody pikes home from the battlefield to use as spindles.

Nor should we forget the vision of the writer on the mist-veiled lake, its truth remained as bright within him as the patch before his eye was black. The church had to come into the village and the silence spoke: stand up! The path moved beath his shoe. It was the carpenter Johann Buben-leb whose door he knocked at one spring day, and who invited him into his lightless room. He shared it with goats that he had saved, and which fed him: deep in the woods, high in the trees, he had built them platforms and bal-conies and heaved them up with ropes so that they could eat bark and leaves and not be seen by the rogues below or scented by their pack of dogs.

But the last few years, with their wet and cold, had tanned his hide too, and tanned his spirits besides. His lungs whistled, and his limbs creaked like old church pews. His planing arm, which had once built proud ships that sailed the seas, he could now hardly lift to the table's edge. His hands lay in his lap like tools from former times whose use no one now knows, and when the author of these lines told him his intentions, his bright eyes froze in the smoke from his cherrywood pipe and he did not even shake his kindly head.

He had suffered much from his youth onwards, he had

been wounded and broken on the wheel with his wife for a few ducats. The Lord had heard barely one of his prayers, he was chased poor and naked into the thorn-bushes, and forced to seek shelter among the dead for the sake of his life. Their pestilential slime had dripped into his panting mouth, his trembling had touched their cold hands and now, when someone came to him and told him what was needed in spite of everything, for this spot on God's earth, he couldn't believe his ears. He drew on his pipe.

It may be that God requires us to make a great effort to receive mildness in return. But how is your tender vision to emerge from the fog, he said at last, how could the holy house in its entirety cross the lake? Though it be consecrated, filled with songs that lift the heart, with mute prayers, with fine scents and flowers: is it not, from threshold to crown, made of stone, not to speak of glass and iron fittings? Would it not sink like a stone? And the water will spill over the shore and drown our cottages with a tidal wave! He waved the thought away and blew the bitter smoke to the roof. – Let the chapel fall where no one wants to live any more, and walk with God, good Bredelin. A time may come when we have strength and pious sense enough to build a new one.

More and more refugees were coming to the farm. They were installing rows of makeshift beds in almost every out-house and even in the byre. Although it was still freezing at night, the horses, including Breeze, had to go to the paddock in the park, and Luisa got hold of an old woollen blanket and tied it around the horse's neck and the base of its tail. Admittedly it was barely putting on any weight, but its hooves seemed to be getting better; already it wasn't walking as hesitantly as before, and the others tolerated it in their midst. Particularly after sunset they stood crammed together, and when Luisa read in her room she could hear the animals coughing in the darkness.

Blue of the sky in the puddles one morning when she cycled to Kluvensiek. The dewdrops on the edges of the thatched roofs sparkled like something perfectly crafted in the early light. By the duck pond she stopped at the Storms' house and pushed her bike into the garden, lean-ing it against the stonewalled oven. The cold bricks smelled like the beech-smoke in which Ole's grandfather hung sausages and fish from the canal. His mother was digging up a flowerbed. 'Hello, Luisa!' she called. 'The boy will be delighted. There's mint tea on the stove.'

She was a wig-maker and worked at home. Through the glass door of her workshop a shelf of cardboard boxes could be seen, with strands of hair spilling from them. On a long table there was a row of different-sized model heads with extremely fine tulle covering and shocks of hair in all possible colours, almost completely woven. Ole was sitting by the kitchen window drawing, and Luisa shook hands with him and wished him a happy birthday. 'If you hurry up getting older you'll soon have caught up with me,' she said, 'and then we can go dancing, can't we? You always wanted to twirl a pretty blonde around the place.'

He laughed shyly, even turned red and shifted sideways so that she would have room on the bench, which was draped with a cowskin. He wore an ironed pair of trousers with turn-ups and a jacket in the same dark brown material, and Luisa dug her present out of her rucksack, *Emil and the Detectives*. Thanks to Frau Mangoldt she now had two copies of the book. 'There are illustrations in it,' she said, because he wasn't especially keen on reading. 'You could copy them out.'

Pleased, he started flicking through it, and she took two cups from the sink and the pot from the stove and filled them with tea. 'That's a nice suit you've got there. Really *schnieke*, as they say in Berlin.'

Straightening his back, he pulled his white shirt collar over his lapel and looked down at himself with a smile. 'Do you think so? Frau Milger made it for me, from my dad's things. Look at this, leather buttons. Unfortunately the lining of the jacket has a blue stain from his Pelikan, but these turn-ups are sensible because I'm growing so quickly . . . These were his Sunday trousers, and I've got two now.'

She felt the fabric, the smooth worsted, between her fingers, and brushed some fluff from his sleeve. 'Doesn't he need them any more?'

The boy pursed his lips and shrugged. 'I don't think so, he's getting his uniform. Seen these?'

Drawing back the lacy curtain he pointed at the figures made of acorns, rose-hips and chestnuts on the windowsill: women with hair made of flax and skirts made of lantern paper, warriors with matchstick arms and spiky helmets, animals with moss coats and horns made of cloves. 'I made these for him,' he said. 'All in the past year, as a Christmas present. But you're not allowed to send them to the front.'

Luisa took a sip from the tepid tea. 'Goodness!' she said. 'You've got talent!'

He pulled a razor blade from his pencil case and nodded seriously. 'Yes,' he replied, 'that's what Grandpa says too. And by the way, do you know why the chestnuts, these ones here, are called horse chestnuts? In the olden days, in the Middle Ages or around then, they only grew in Asia. But when the Turks invaded Europe they always had a sack of them as medicine for their war-horses. Because they were important. If they got a cold or went lame, they were given a handful of those, and off they went!'

He sharpened a red pencil, and Luisa set her cup down, surprised. 'Well then it makes sense that they didn't call them cow chestnuts or something, doesn't it? Where do you find them? Here in the village?'

He shook his head. 'These are from the lake, where the

oldest trees grow,' he said and looked quickly at the door. 'But we're not allowed to go there any more, it's forbidden. They have dogs and they shoot. Or else you're locked up – even if you only know there was someone there and didn't report it. Why are you asking?'

The tea was very sweet, and Luisa licked her lips and said: 'Because I want some too, simple as that. Will you help me look?'

He opened his eyes wide. 'But, Luisa, you collect chestnuts in the autumn! Then they're beautiful and shiny and very firm. You'll only find wrinkled ones now. What do you want to do with them? Make things too?'

'I'll tell you if you show me the trees, you little fraidy-cat.'

Laughing, he shaded in the curls of the girl in the Pony Hats advertisement. 'What's a fraidy-cat?'

After she had explained it to him, they finished their tea, fetched their bikes and cycled down the village street and into the forest. The oaks that grew here were very old, cracked and peeled by wind and weather, whose branches had a look of stubborn fury. But even at the first crossroads there was a slender chestnut tree with gleaming, glazed-looking buds, and Luisa jumped from her bike. She swept the grass with the tip of her shoe and collected the fruits from the previous year.

She didn't find many. Ole, who wore a tattered wax jacket over his suit, held her rucksack open, and after they had crossed a ploughed field on the harvest route, they cycled on beneath tall pine trees that leant slightly towards the east. While the treetops caught the sun, the lower parts of the trees had a growth of moss, and the bark had been stripped from some and the wood carved with a fish-bone pattern: that way the resin could drip into tins hanging below.

Lorry or tractor tracks on the unpaved road, and again and again the trunks revealed a view of a high wire fence with arched posts and porcelain insulators. Signs hung on it a good twenty metres apart, and on all of them, in the same clumsy style – it made her think of lino-cuts at school – the same skull and crossbones was depicted. 'Halt! Danger zone!' it said beneath the bones, whose red paint was already fading. 'Shots will be fired without warning!'

With the tip of his tongue between his lips, Ole slowed down. He seemed to be looking for something among the young pine trees that were now growing along the ditch. It was a plantation, not yet thinned, and he pressed a hand on the top of the bell and turned off down a deer track. After a few metres they dismounted and leaned their bikes against a tree stump with a salt block nailed to it. 'We need to be very careful,' Ole whispered. 'My cousin, Liebgard, was mushrooming here once, and she was brought home in a black car. And her mum spanked her bottom.'

The path rose slightly, the young trees grew so densely that at first you could only see the sky. After only a few steps dewdrops wetted Luisa's coat, the branches with the nut-sized cones that she clung to were sticky. Red berries gleamed here and there in the deer droppings, and at last they reached a slope and were able to look between seashell concrete posts and down into the dip and all the way to the lake. Birch trees were reflected in its black water, and Luisa was surprised: on an old map in the foyer of the convent, where it was called 'Mare Innocentiae', it had looked enormous. But it was no bigger than the Schreventeich in Kiel.

Wooden huts in front of the edge of the forest opposite, a watchtower looming over their roofs, and countless people worked in the ditches along the shore. Guarded by soldiers with carbines, they wore grey uniforms dirty to the knee and they were picking peat from the moor, in brick-sized pieces. They loaded them on sleds and dragged them up over a confusion of planks and logs to a square by the fence, where they were stacked in an airy lattice structure. It was all done in great haste, at a lick, with a clatter of runners and clogs, and Luisa closed her eyes for a moment.

Her saliva tasted as sour as the smell around here, and when she quietly asked Ole who the people were he shrugged and whispered: 'Don't know, probably prisoners. Your chestnuts are over there.'

Partridges flew up from rotten brown bracken. The old trees, two dozen or more, might once have been the beginning or the end of an avenue; now fences had been stapled to the scaly trunks, row after row, a hand's breadth apart. Tufts of fur or hair hung on the barbs, a tattered glove, and the cobbles that could be made out in the grass led to a small chapel overgrown with ivy and scrub.

It too was part of the camp boundary: wire had been stretched over the crumbling mud wall and nailed to the half-timbering; the window towards the forest was bricked up. The belfry with the empty bell-frame had lost its pointed tip, a gutter hung down, but the rusty corrugated-iron roof seemed to be watertight, because the space was used as a storeroom. Beneath the semi-circular lintel, carved with words in Latin, a stack of boxes and canisters could be seen. They were also piled up on the pews, and in one of the wall niches, normally reserved for a saint or eternal light, there was a helmet.

Two trucks stopped outside the huts by the shore, peat was loaded on, and the children slipped through the spring leaves looking for chestnuts, but here again they didn't find many. Barely a single one was hard, some felt as if they were hollow, maggots crawled from others, and they threw them into the rucksack – when all of a sudden they smelled cigarettes, sweetish smoke, and heard a cracking sound nearby. The young pine trees leapt into motion, drops of water jumped from the needles, and suddenly a soldier was standing in front of them, with his carbine aimed at them. 'Halt!' said another one, who was leading a sheepdog. 'What are you doing here?'

Like their coats, the men's forage caps were green, and for a moment the children stayed silent and stared at the muzzled dog. The fur on its chest and hindquarters was black with moisture, and it kept rearing up on its short leash. It wasn't barking, but its panting rose to a wheeze that made Luisa think its breath must be seething hot. Slobber spilled from the leather mesh, and Ole said: 'We're just looking for mushrooms.'

The soldier with the carbine came closer. 'In spring? Now that makes me curious. Which mushrooms are growing at this time of year? Let's see!' With the barrel in the hollow of his elbow, he took the rucksack from Luisa, reached in and looked at a handful of the soil-covered fruits. 'These look like chestnuts to me.'

'Yes, we're collecting them too,' she said quickly. 'For the horses up at the farm. They have a cough.'

The other soldier, who had a holster in his belt, wrapped the leather leash tighter around his fist and said: 'You don't believe that yourselves! You're spying! Where's your camera?'

'We haven't got one,' Ole replied. 'We really are just looking for mushrooms. St George's mushroom grows around now, and so does deer truffle, which is good for colds. And if you're lucky you'll also find morels. I don't suppose we can go now?'

The solder with the carbine let the chestnuts fall back into the rucksack and examined the front pocket, which contained a small knife and two yellow winter apples. 'Can't you read what it says on the signs? Where do you live? What does your father do?'

Blanching beneath his severe gaze, Ole looked at the ground. 'He's a soldier too,' he said softly. 'In Hungary, with the Panzergrenadiers. He's been wounded three times and he got a lot of medals and decorations, even the Iron Cross second class. I can show you. As proof, I mean.'

The guard, who disguised the hint of a grin with a severe frown, raised his chin and asked, 'Really? Do you wear it around your neck or something, little man?'

Ole laughed awkwardly, a bit of snot bursting from his nose. 'I don't. I wouldn't be allowed to. His captain sent it to us in Kluvensiek, with the telegram. As well as the close combat clasp and the other decorations, the stars. Mum wept with joy. They'd just get dirty at the front, wouldn't they?'

He turned his head as if he had also asked the question to Luisa, and the soldier darted a quick glance at the dog handler. Then he reached out his arm and plucked a withered pine needle from the child's hair. 'Yes, that's an idea, you might be right,' he said, his face assuming a milder expression.

He gave the rucksack back to Luisa and pointed to the path between the young trees. 'And now clear off. You have no business here!'

*

First stars in the sky, a half-moon, still a deep orange, with the gable of the dairy outlined against it, its glazed clay battlements. The ladder at the byre was long with sagging rails, and Luisa closed her eyes and took a deep breath before climbing the next rung. The farmhouse opposite was in darkness, the only candles burning in the attic, in the kitchen. Billie was curling her mother's hair. On the table, small glasses of green liqueur.

The wind smelled of ashes, and when she was finally standing on the platform, beneath the brow of the thatch, she was able to look out over the sheds to the banks of the Alte Eider. Beyond the forest there had been a raid an hour before, and the sawmill in Rade and some fir trees were burning. Further to the east people and carts could be seen, a dark procession against the shimmering water, and although they were far away and not even the sound of horses' hooves reached her, Luisa thought she could hear a baby crying.

The door below the crown of the building was unlocked. There were a dozen dorm rooms for workers up here, all empty since the last recruitment drive. There was no lamp in the narrow corridor, but some light shone between the cracks in the floorboards. The evening milking had begun, the tap of the one-legged stool on the stone floor, and in the lowing of some of the cows one could hear the impatience, the painful desire to be next. The jets of milk rattled loudly into the buckets and grew gradually quieter.

Someone was whistling a popular song, it sounded as if he was standing on the hay floor directly beneath her, and Luisa walked as cautiously as possible so as not to be noticed. Only an oil cloth hung in front of the moonlit room that she stepped into, which had a similar dormer to her own on the other side of the yard. A tiny table, a chair with a seat of ragged straw and an iron bed stood under the oval window. A bare light bulb hung above the mirror, and on the enamelled tin wash basin there was a piece of blue soap, almost new; the imprinted trademark, a stagecoach, could still be felt under the fingertips.

No cross, no photograph, no sign of a magazine or book. In the open wardrobe an oilskin jacket, steel-capped shoes below it, and Luisa sat down on the bed, the red corduroy velvet bedspread, and looked across through the linden tree to the farmhouse. The clock tower was boxed in with boards, the chimney was smoking, and she gave a start when a light suddenly came on behind her window and for a heartbeat she saw her own silhouette.

It was Billie who was peering into the room and seemed to be looking for something, and when the light bulb went out again Luisa was embarrassed to think that from this vantage-point Walter could not only make out her shelf, with the paperbacks and the gilded spines: in a niche between her dictionaries there was also the tattered brown teddy-bear from her childhood days, one of its paws darned, and glittering on her bedside table was the musical clock with the ballerina. It was broken and actually belonged to her sister.

She hunched on the bed, pushed her folded hands between her thighs and closed her eyes. It was comfortable and warm here, above the cows; it smelled of hay and creamy milk, and a faintly musty smell recalling autumn leaves or mushrooms flowed from the old thatch above her. And when she pressed her nose into the pillow, which she only dared to do after hesitating for a while and only through the bedspread, behind the scent of Walter's pomade she noticed another, sharper smell that made her eyes damp and her throat dry, and for which she had no words – only one, which struck her as strange, and which her sister would have mocked. She thought the pillow truly had a smell about it.

She lay there for half an hour or thereabouts, and almost went to sleep. Then carefully, on tiptoes, she left the attic and went out onto the landing. It was a clear, starry night, in which a flutter of wings could be heard, and the distant trumpeting of cranes, and she checked that there was no one in the yard before she slowly climbed back down the rungs; they were dangerously smooth from the milk-fat on the workers' hands. And in the middle of the ladder she suddenly paused, rubbed her eyes with her sleeve and whispered: 'Why are you crying, you silly cow? Don't start crying again! This is how life is now.'

*

It was still light the next time her father came back from Kiel. He was driving a different car from his usual one, a green VW utility vehicle with a sand-coloured soft top. 'It's actually watertight,' he said, because it had been raining all day. 'Generals are now charging about behind the front line in my lovely Mercedes. I'll get it back riddled with bullet-holes, if I ever see it again. Anyway, the tank was almost empty and the tyres hardly had any tread. Give me a hand, please.'

The package he handed Luisa was about the size of a shoebox. He himself was carrying a suitcase and a bulging rucksack, and while they climbed the stairs to the attic she breathlessly told him that she had brought a bull calf into the world, a black one, which was still a bit thin but whose little horn-stumps were already developing. She also mentioned its name, and he laughed out loud under his burden and had a coughing fit that made his face red. Her mother was looking through the corrugated-glass oval and opened the door. 'What's up with you two?' she asked and indicated to them with a roll of the eyes that there was someone else in the kitchen. 'Do you have to smell like that in the middle of the day?'

Gudrun was standing by the stove and nodded to them, and Luisa's father whistled through his teeth. She wasn't wearing the usual woollen jacket and pleated skirt, but a close-fitting suit of dark-blue raw silk, a white blouse with a tulip collar showing between its lapels. Her glossy dyed-blonde hair was shaped at the back of her head into a long roll, known as a 'banana', she was wearing lipstick and she smiled when she noticed Luisa's expression of open-mouthed astonishment. 'We're off to see the Grand Admiral . . .'

Her gold chain bracelet rattled against the pot that she was stirring, and bubbles burst in a spinach-like brew. 'So, Mum, that should be enough. You apply that under your ribs in the evening and leave it to work for twenty minutes. You've probably just got gallstones, like Grandma. It's not serious, you can live with it. Drink a bit less coffee, cut out fat, and if it gets really bad . . .' She looked at the sideboard cupboard, and moved a few tubes and boxes. The heels of her pumps were twice as high as those of the 'Trommler' shoes she usually wore. 'Didn't I bring you a bottle of aspirin?'

Her mother, wearing loose black trousers and a Danish pullover, slumped in the stained wing chair and struck a match. Tobacco had trickled from the cigarette and the empty roll of paper flared. 'You did, my love, and for that I will be eternally grateful to you,' she said flatly. 'I've been puzzling for days about where they might be, not least because of my arthritis; often the pain is almost unbearable. But they've vanished into thin air.'

Gudrun pressed on the pump handle with her elbow, washed her hands under the tap and said with a chuckle: 'Well, who knows, perhaps the master of the house secretly swallowed them all?' She pointed at the table, at the schnapps and wine bottles standing on it. 'Or what do you do when you have your daily hangover? Hair of the dog?'

Her stepfather hung his jacket over a chair. 'Me? I go in search of a nice little pussycat,' he murmured and looked at his wife. 'How's Billie getting on?'

She exhaled smoke and waved a dismissive hand. 'How do you expect, with that stupid thing she's got . . . as long as it doesn't get into her kidneys. Yesterday her urine was almost red. I'm keen to know what the doctor in Sehestedt will say; I don't trust him. Whether you're a human being, a cow or a horse, you always get those little round tablets, they call them globes or something. God knows what's in them. But if they deport him we're going to have big problems.'

Gudrun took a dishcloth off the oven rail. 'Oh, come on, it won't be as bad as that,' she replied and dried her hands. 'Still, my dear sister can go on scampering about the place and make eyes at the foreign workers, from what I hear . . . The women up at the villa have already been telling me what a flibbertigibbet she is. She's always sitting in the Fährhof, joking with the guards from the . . . Watch out, Mum, your ash!'

She held out a saucer, and Luisa's father, who had been putting some jars of preserves in the cupboard, looked around. He was still sweating from climbing the stairs, his light-blue shirt collar was damp, but his voice sounded cold when he said: 'Just for general information, madam: my daughter is not a flibbertigibbet! Could you please inform your friends to that effect?'

Apparently startled, Gudrun checked the position of her earrings, droplet-shaped pearls. 'Of course, you're completely right,' she replied. 'They aren't my friends, either. I'm just repeating what I've heard. And I wouldn't take it so seriously, Dad, you know what those officers' wives are like. All those years without a husband . . . They can hardly wait for victory.'

Shaking his head, he opened a bottle of cognac. 'Billie is a tomboy,' he insisted. 'You can't stick her in the corner with a book like our little rascal here. She wants to wear smart clothes and skate across the parquet in dancing shoes, not wade through mud in wellington boots. Here she is spending the best days of her life in the absence of everything, and the last thing she needs is someone calling her a flibbertigibbet!'

Gudrun, her cheeks inflated, raised her hands and moved them as if a powerful gust of wind were pushing her downwards. 'That's enough, Dad, calm down. Nice and calm. We're all making sacrifices these days, you don't need to get quite so *échauffé*!'

Her mother frowned. 'What don't we need to get?'

Luisa sat on the arm of the chair. 'It's French,' she answered. 'The language of the enemy. But it's in *Effi Briest*. I think it means "getting yourself all worked up".'

'Exactly,' Gudrun said. 'Always keep a cool head. And a sober one too, not least for the sake of your health.' She smiled at her stepfather. 'Do you really have to drink so much, by the way?'

He looked past her out of the rain-drenched window and closed his eyes for a moment. 'No, of course not. I don't have to do anything at all,' he replied after an irritable-sounding sigh. 'But I want to, imagine that! I enjoy it. And besides, I'm a restaurateur. What would people think of a butcher who only ate porridge?'

Then he took a sip of brandy straight from the bottle, winked at his youngest and pointed at the package that she had put on the table. 'That's for you, my sweet, by the way. I got it from the ruins of a house. Every room looted, even the handles from the doors and windows were gone, only the books were left. They're a bit scorched, but it's all legible, even between the lines.'

He sat down at the table with a grin, and Luisa kissed him on the cheek and cut the string. Seven reddish-brown cloth-bound books with woven roses and faded gold edges were wrapped in packing paper, all by the same author. She didn't know either the strange names or how to pronounce them, and looked at him quizzically. 'Well, Shakespeare,' he said, 'William, the Great. Never heard of him?'

She shook her head and flicked through the books, which smelled of cold ashes. There were deckle-edged family photographs between the pages, a shopping list written in a shaky hand, old bread-ration cards and pressed flowers. 'But it's . . . Is it English?' she asked, disappointed. 'I can't read it.'

Her father shrugged. 'No? Then learn it. Start straight away. If I read the situation correctly it's about to come in useful.' He looked up at the lamp, a bowl full of dead flies, and tugged reflectively at his neck, the fading skin. And after clearing his throat he took a breath and declaimed in

English: 'We are such stuff / As dreams are made on; and our little life / Is rounded with a sleep.'

Then he took another swig of the brandy, and Luisa, who had of course understood not a word and yet everything, probably because of his voice and the sad echo it found in her heart, was about to ask him to repeat the quotation, when Gudrun said, 'No, no! Not like that!'

She raised a finger, and moved it up and down as she might have done in her classrooms. 'I think it's quite impossible of you, Dad, to instil such things in the child. Of course an engagement with Englishness, with that country's language and literature – which is in itself only the expression of a Nordic-Teutonic attitude of mind – makes a valuable contribution to the training of our young people. But we will always speak German in this Gau, that much is clear. Our troops are defeating the enemy as we speak! I have reliable information.'

Her stepfather drew a Flor del Arte from his waistcoat pocket and removed the paper. 'Of course,' he replied. 'And our dingleberries will soon be gilded by the Pope. You shouldn't always believe what your husband tells you.' He raised the cigar to his ear and rolled it between his fingers. Then he bit off the tip and spat it on the floor. 'Pay more heed to his silence.'

His wife turned around, tutting, and glared at him. 'Wilhelm!' she exclaimed. 'Are you really so far gone? What does that have to do with her husband?'

Gudrun, a white shadow having passed across her face, held both hands in front of her belly, the gentle swell. With the tip of her shoe she pushed the little lump of tobacco into a crack between the floorboards. 'Yes, I'm wondering the same thing myself right now,' she said. 'What are you suggesting? What would he be keeping from me?'

Her stepfather rummaged in a matchbox, almost crushing it between his clumsy fingers, but said nothing. Her pale blue eyes with the delicate veins running through the white seemed to bulge slightly as she waited for his answer. At the same time she looked at her mother, who just pulled a face and waved a hand, a wordless, 'Don't listen! You know him, after all,' and swathed herself in smoke.

But her eldest, lips pressed together, chin trembling and wrinkled, would not be reassured. She stepped to the table, tapped both thumbs on the edge and lowered her curved forehead, which gave her face a menacing quality. 'No, I would like to know now, thank you!' she said. 'As far as I'm concerned you can get drunk every day if you don't care too much about your life, but you must pay attention to what you say, Dad! What is he hiding from me? What do you think? Affairs? Don't worry, I'm quite aware that he's important, that he has influence. I see the covetous glances. But I have claws too, believe me . . .'

Luisa's father sucked the little flame into the cigar. The tobacco crackled, and he puffed for a long time before blowing out the match. Down below, in the administrator's office, the telephone rang shrilly and Motte barked. 'Nonsense!' he murmured at last, in a strangely hoarse voice, but didn't look at his stepdaughter. As the smoke spilled from his mouth, he studied the ember. 'Who's saying anything of the sort? Your Vinzent knows what he's got in you, he's not an idiot. I just meant that he is still wrapping himself in silence with regard to our wishes or those of the girls. Does their time here count as a land-girl year, or not? Couldn't you do some digging? Otherwise they might end up in the further reaches of Wallachia hoeing weeds!'

He darted a glance at his wife, who pursed her lips almost imperceptibly, and Gudrun exhaled noisily. She did up the buttons – oval, attached with gold thread – of her jacket, straightened the collar of her blouse and said, 'Oh yes, that dreary business . . . Yes, I'd almost forgotten. I don't know whether that still falls under his area of responsibility, but you're right, we should sort that out, if necessary with the BDM. I'll leave him a note.'

In fact Louisa had no objection to a year in a strange environment, maybe even abroad, and she was about to say so when the sound of a car horn rang out in the yard, an elegant tritone, and her stepsister looked out of the window. 'Well excuse me, speak of the Devil!' she murmured and touched the roll of hair on the back of her head, making her hairpins more secure. 'By the way, you'll be getting the official invitation to his party. The printer has been going through a difficult time, and has to make the ink himself. Out of soot and oak galls, imagine!'

She slipped into her coat, waved to everyone and was walking to the door when a shadow appeared, a reddish one, and at that moment the handle lowered just as she was about to reach for it. Hesitating, she drew in her chin and took a step back. Again she held her hands over her belly.

Sibylle, scarf and rain-cape over her arm, with the collar of her blouse open to the neck of her bodice, had fiery cheeks and droplets of sweat on her upper lip and was clearly not surprised by her stepsister's presence, although she was by her elegance. She too emitted a whistle, or at least the breath for a whistle.

Gudrun lowered her eyes and studied her from her tousled hair, which stuck out in every possible direction like copper spirals, to her dark red stockings and suede shoes. One lace was untied. 'My, my,' she said, and her nostrils twitched and the wrinkle in her forehead deepened. 'I thought you were with that Jewish doctor. Are you wearing a new perfume again?'

'Not at all,' Billie said, walked past her and threw her things over the hook. 'It just seems that way to you.' Smiling, she winked at Luisa and opened the door to the bathroom. 'It's my boyfriend's aftershave.'

*

Tracer fire could now sometimes be seen at night, and in the pale light over the landscape one seemed to be in a different present, a space without boundaries and names, in which the shadows of the trees churned and those of the gables crept like saw-teeth across the fields. But in the morning everything was the same as usual, and when Luisa had had breakfast, read for a while and learned a few words of English, she helped the refugees to make mattresses. Many children were working in the straw barn: some climbed up to the space under the roof and threw down the sheaves, others untied the twine and plucked out the beards. Then the stalks were chopped up with the spade and thrown into the draught so that the chaff and dust could blow away. The chopped straw was stuffed into jute bags which were sewn up with thick threads.

It was hard work, the air stung their eyes, their sweaty skin itched, and when Luisa washed herself at the pump beside the chicken coop someone tapped her on the back. The fair-haired boy, with his trouser bottoms tucked into his socks, wore a cap with a brim and a battered coat with toggles and held out his hand. 'Want to buy?'

A little taller than her, he was about her age. She had seen him quite often over the last few days; the family lived in the old stable, his mother was the one with the stump. The two Kleber brothers waited behind him in their Hitler Youth uniforms: Hubert, with a hunting knife in his belt, had his fists braced against his hips, and Alfred, the smaller one, was absently picking his nose as he stared at the chicken wire full of feathers, the sunlight passing through the fluff.

Her chin dripping, Luisa leaned forward. Quivering, two hairless mice cowered on the boy's palm. Newly born and taken from one of the many nests beneath the sheaves, the painfully red animals were smaller than her smallest finger. They still had no ears and only stumpy tails, and although their lids were closed, their dark eyes could be seen moving back and forth beneath the skin. Luisa sniffed. 'Why should I buy them?'

'Why not?' said the boy, and his thin-lipped grin looked older than he was. 'You're Jews, after all.'

She shook her fingers dry. 'What are we? How do you work that out?'

'Red-heads are Jews. And your sister's a tart as well.

One mark each, or ten cigarettes. You can also pay in instalments. If you don't buy the mice . . .' He closed his dirty hand around the animals and pointed over his shoulder with his thumb. '. . . the cats'll get them.'

There were lots of cats on the farm, particularly in the half-dilapidated buildings behind the dairy, and she took a step towards him. He smelled of the disinfectant used to clean the stables and sheds before the animals were moved in. 'You look the type. You're completely off your head! Get the hell out of here and don't let me see you again or you'll get a kick in the pants. I don't do deals with bigheads.'

The boy hesitated and wrinkled his nose. 'Why, what do you mean?'

'Well, you of course! Boys with blue eyes are bigheads, everyone knows that,' Luisa said. 'Otherwise their eyes would be green or brown.'

He took off his cap, wiped a strand of hair off his forehead and looked around at the others. 'Is that true, what the *schickse* says? Have I got blue eyes?'

The brothers came closer and studied his face. Hubert shrugged, the other boy drew the corners of his mouth down, and now their spokesman got the joke. There was loud cackling behind the wire, and he narrowed his eyelids and said through his teeth: 'Well, no, then, you Jewish whore. You'll see . . .'

And before the girl could grab his arm he had lifted it up and thrown the tiny creatures, almost transparent in the sunlight, over the fence in a high arc. They fell amongst the whitish droppings, where, after a brief hesitation and curious craning of necks by the chickens, a storm of beaks and claws descended on them. And the boys ran laughing away.

*

Since the last air-raid the swastika flags had been stored in the tarred box beside the flagpole, to avoid provoking the pilots. It also contained the big banner of the Reich Food Authority, embroidered with a sword and an ear of corn, crafted by the Women's League, and when Luisa crossed the yard with her jug Herr Thamling was spreading a sheet over it, a white one. To protect the precious fabric from the dust, as he explained with a grin.

Her mother was still asleep, and she took the pot off the stove and stirred a spoonful of sugar into the colostrum, with its faint scent of vanilla. Then she knocked at the door bearing the signed photograph of Zarah Leander, but her sister didn't answer. When she entered the darkened room, she was met by a wave of warm air; glowing in the corner of the little cork-lined room was the heating coil that her father had brought her from Kiel. 'Shut the door!' cried Billie, only her shock of hair showing above the eiderdown. 'There's a draught!'

There were illustrated magazines all over the place, particularly Danish ones, even though she couldn't read them, but also *Faith and Beauty* and *Girls in Service*. The wardrobe was open, linen spilled from the dresser with all kinds of make-up on it, and shirts and stockings hung even from the lamp on the wall. Luisa pushed the alarm clock, the ashtray and the bottle of Prontosil tablets aside and set the milk down on the bedside table. 'From a cow that just gave birth,' she said. 'It gives you strength. How are you? Do you have a temperature?'

With a groan her sister pulled herself up on the bed-post. 'No, don't think so. It just hurts. It's a really nasty pain, particularly after peeing. As if you had a handful of broken glass in your belly. It's not something you would wish on your worst enemy.' She gave a pained smile. 'Well, maybe some of your relatives, for half an hour.'

Luisa pulled the curtain aside. The sun shone through the perfume bottles by the mirror, and her mother's buckled shoes gleamed under the chair, and she said, 'You're a terrible one, you know. You've got to stop.'

The other girl stuffed pillows behind her back. 'Oh right, is it time for Sunday school again? And what exactly am I supposed to stop, Mother Superior?'

'Don't act so innocent, you know very well!' Luisa said. 'Sooner or later Gudrun will find out, and then . . . People already think you're flighty.'

Billie sniffed the milk and looked at the shoes with a frown. 'Are they still here?' she murmured. 'I told Mum I didn't want them.' Then she took a sip and set the cup down on her belly. 'And why do they think I'm flighty? Because I paint my nails and make my lips red, or what? Well excuse me, let them, those potato-heads. They have no idea what living is! Where other people have dreams, they have sausages or Knight's Crosses. But I want something else, do you see that?'

Luisa nodded, but she had barely been listening. She wrapped a tendril of hair around her finger as she looked out of the window, into the little park with the paddock, the dilapidated tea-house and the flute-playing faun on its mossy plinth. Her throat was dry, and she swallowed and moved her lips a few times before she said: 'I don't want to know what you're getting up to with Vinzent, even though I don't think it's right. It's your business. But be honest: have you done it with Walter as well?'

Her sister took another drink and groaned quietly with contentment. 'With who?' she asked into the cup. 'Which Walter?'

Luisa turned around and gazed penetratingly into her face. 'Are you serious? You were in his room above the stable! He was wearing pyjama trousers and a sort of gym vest: the big milker with the green eyes and the lovely teeth. He has a voice like Dad's, only a bit more silvery.'

'Ha!' Billie smiled broadly. 'So you're already taking in every detail about the boys? Well, soon they'll be setting their caps at you, just you wait. But now I know who you mean; his name's Walter, that's right. A good, strong fellow, the animals like him. But too respectable and elo-quent, if you ask me, too nice. Men shouldn't be like that, it makes them boring very quickly. After all, we ourselves are angels, aren't we?' She dabbed some milk skin from her chin. 'We need someone with horns.'

Then she set the cup back down on the bedside table. 'And anyway he's got a girlfriend, one of those girls from Danzig in the coaching inn, Elisabeth. They're even engaged, I think. – And by the way, do you know what the doctor called what I've got? Honeymoon cystitis. It sounds almost as funny as it's painful. A honeymoon inflamma-tion. That'd be nice.' She sank under the eiderdown again with a yawn. 'Will you take those shoes with you when you go?'

Luisa said nothing. She pulled up the zip of her pullover and stared at the heater, a dented metal box, which creaked from time to time. In the sun it was impossible to tell whether the element inside was getting any power, it was more brown than red. But its heat was apparent each time floating bits of fluff or dust suddenly burned up above it.

*

The windowsill was cracked and had crumbled away in places, and the glass vibrated. The cross-shaped shadow of the plane sent the horses trotting to the edge of the paddock. The bomb bay was open, only two of the four propellers were working, and black smoke poured from the shattered gun turret beneath the tail. At a steep angle, as if preparing to fly in a curve, the plane brushed the trees along the avenue with the tip of a wing; but the noise of the engines drowned out the breaking and splintering of the branches.

A wheel came away from the landing gear, struck the road and leapt back into the air, and then the Halifax with the cloud-coloured camouflage paint was out of sight, and Luisa waited for a crash or an explosion, a column of fire like that time in Kiel. But nothing happened, the smoke was dispersed in the evening wind, and the slight quiver beneath their feet – it was easy to imagine. She slipped into her coat and ran down the steps and fetched her bicycle from the barn.

The air smelled of kerosene. Two lorries, both box

wagons, and a black Horch sped past the farm; children charged out of lots of buildings and leapt over fences and ditches to get to the Eider meadows more quickly. Cartridge belts hung in the linden trees, tattered parachute silk, a red beret, and already two women had rolled the broken-off tyre into the yard and were using kitchen knives to cut sole-size pieces from the rubber.

Old Thamling overtook Luisa on his clattering BMW; the road to the canal was filled with curious people. The bomber had ripped a wide trench full of grass and scrubby roots in the calf-grazing pasture called the Spielkoppel. It was sunk on one side, one wing loomed in the air at an angle, the other lay in pieces beside the airframe. Behind the windows of the convent, which had only just escaped disaster, the nuns and their patients jostled; white bandages gleamed in the dusk.

The two trucks and the limousine parked in front of the stepped gable. Some men, many of them quite elderly, armed with forks and hunting rifles, formed a semicircle around the smoking plane, from which the sound of radio signals could still be heard: a hum, a rattle, a beep. With the broad armband of the Volkssturm on their sleeves, they refused to let anyone climb over the wire fences, because not all the people who had turned up were onlookers. Many held wire-cutters or hacksaws.

Accompanied by marines, Vinzent, wearing his black Hauptsturmführer jacket, inspected the wreck with its British cockades. There were large-calibre bullet-holes everywhere. The massive Plexiglas nose, with a machine-gun barrel protruding from it, was smeared with blood on the inside, but in the cockpit above it a pilot could be seen. With his helmet against the back of his neck and his sweat-drenched temple pressed against the side window, he seemed to be staring at the river, where broken propeller blades drifted on the eddies. Luisa even thought she could see a smile on his white face, a smile of surprise. The shadow of a seagull passed over him.

Vinzent's high boots, the seams of his black jodhpurs and the holster on his belt were all shiny and new, and even though he had never fought at the front he wore several decorations and badges of honour and the red ribbon of the Iron Cross in his buttonhole. He strode around the frame, over strips of churned-up grass and bits of rubble, and hammered with the handle of his loose-weave whip against the aluminium, which seemed to be very thin; the steel ribs showed under the paint. 'Out of there!' he called in German, and then in English: 'Come on!'

Smoke and white flakes of ash blew over the river. Onlookers stood on the opposite bank as well; dyke-workers, leaning on their shovels, spoke in foreign languages. Someone coughed, a groan rang out inside the wreck, a long-drawn-out lament, and Vinzent took a step back and rested his hand on his holster. The soldiers raised their carbines, the safety catches clicked, and then for a moment it was so quiet that the wind could be heard in the bullet-holes, a metallic whistle. Charred scraps of insulating material were thrown into the grass and a man was crawling out of the open bomb bay.

Luisa pushed her bicycle towards the administrator's BMW. He was sitting, legs spread, behind the fuel tank, his heels on the cobbles, and taking out his meerschaum pipe. 'Now our lovely pasture's buggered on top of everything,' he said. 'By the time clover that doesn't taste of petrol grows there again, the summer will be over.' He opened a greasy leather bag and took out some tobacco. 'Should you even be here, little one? I think you're better off with your books.'

She pointed to the Englishman, whose blond hair was sticky with some reddish-brown substance. After they had helped him up he leaned against the hull of the plane, panting heavily. A soldier patted down his green overalls, another handed him a field flask, and after he had drunk some of the water he poured some more into the hollow of his hand and washed the blood out of his eyes.

'What will happen to him now?'

Thamling, filling his pipe, shrugged and murmured: 'That's not up to me, sadly. I'd send him home, to his mother and her teapot. But bombers like him have left our cities in ruins, so people aren't going to be very lenient with the crew. If he's unlucky . . .' He took his storm-proof lighter out of his pocket and clicked the wheel with his thumb. 'But maybe he'll be lucky.'

The sun was low in the sky, Luisa screened her eyes with her hand. The man, more of a boy, had sticking-out ears and pleasantly crooked features, and from a distance he looked awkward and exhausted, but she also thought she could see that he was relieved to have survived the crash and possibly the whole war. An amulet gleamed in the collar of his uniform. 'Dad said there's an agreement that the Führer signed as well,' she whispered. 'You have to treat prisoners decently, with humanity.'

Thamling puffed on his pipe. 'Correct, that's the Geneva Convention. When my comrades and I were taken prisoner in the last war it was still called the Hague Land War Convention. And the humanity of the French consisted in making us work like pit-ponies and taking our boots for their soldiers. Barefoot in the frost by the barbed wire, we asked the citizens of Toulon for bread.' He smiled wearily. 'And they spat in our faces.'

Two marines with blue ribbons on their caps leaned a ladder against the hull and climbed up it. With the stocks of their rifles they knocked in the cockpit and its metal struts, cut through the belts and dragged the dead man into the light. After they had looked through his uniform as well, they pushed him into the grass, where he landed like a sack. They did the same with the corpse in the dorsal turret, both of whose hands had been torn off; he clattered down the aluminium, and when he fell on his back on the ground blood poured from his nose and mouth. Then they destroyed the instrument panel and the switches, and broke the aerials off the roof, and the beeping and humming inside fell silent.

Vinzent, still holding his whip in his left hand, pressed his fists against his hips. His shoulder muscles stood out under his tight black jacket, and he jutted his chin to reveal his row of lower teeth as he addressed the boy. The boy looked up at him with wide eyes and again blood ran from his hair, a thin trickle. It dripped from his forehead onto his uniform when he nodded, and then again when he shook his head. Vinzent reached into the pocket of his riding trousers and held out a white package to him.

Luisa recognized the familiar writing. The Englishman looked quickly at his dead comrade, ran the tip of his tongue over his lips and pulled a cigarette out of the silver paper. The glass of his watch was shattered, from far off it looked like a round piece of ice, his fingers trembled, and one of the soldiers standing nearby reached out his arm and gave him a light. The mouthpiece of the Juno was red from the first drag.

Vinzent pushed his whip into the leg of his boot. With the leather-rimmed cap pushed out of his forehead, he pointed to the field hospital behind them, to the bandaged men and the nuns in the windows. He clapped him on the back, gave an inviting movement of the head and led him around the pile of earth that the bow of the bomber had thrown up. And when the boy hesitated and looked over at the road, at the curious women, children and old people lining it, he grabbed him apparently gently by the back of the neck. With his other hand he opened his holster and, quickly and eagerly, his cheeks hollow, the Englishman took another puff on the cigarette. As he did so he stared at the ground, the fresh grass, the first yellow crocuses.

Some of the forced labourers on the opposite side of the river – probably Russians, because they wore felt boots and fur caps – crossed themselves with their thumbs on forehead, chin and chest. Behind the dented fuselage, where the field sloped down towards the shore, to the faded reeds with the half-gnawed spikes, the two men could no longer be seen, and the administrator, with one foot on the pedal, leaned his torso back and energetically started the BMW. 'What was that?' Luisa asked and looked at him.

With his pipe between his teeth, Thamling put his foot on the accelerator and made the engine rattle. 'A car back-firing!' he exclaimed. 'This bucket is almost as old as me, it belongs on the scrapheap. Now you get home, child. There's an evening milking today.' Then he drove off.

*

On some of the gables of the dilapidated farmhouses on the far side of the avenue it was possible to make out coats of arms or dates, and only the stable built in 1811 still had its roof intact. The thatch was thickly covered in moss, but the twenty heavy cobs that had once stood beneath it, Hafling-ers for the most part, had long ago been deployed as artillery horses at the front. A refugee family now lived in each of the spacious boxes, with lines full of clothes and household goods stretching over them.

Someone was playing the accordion; the air was thick and hard to breathe. The people crouched by the smoking wood stoves, stirring pots and pans and looking around at her over their shoulders. A little boy raised his hands as if he was holding a camera, pressed an invisible shutter release, and Luisa smiled. Even though they were a bit too big she was wearing her mother's buckled shoes, and for the first time she had lined the edges of her eyelids and painted her reddish eyelashes black.

She knocked at the door of the coaching inn. The cry of the children behind it fell silent. The woman who opened to the door to her wasn't much bigger than she was and possibly as old as Billie, nineteen or twenty. She wore a brightly coloured headscarf, a sleeveless apron over her pullover and gym trousers, which were tucked into old rubber boots. Behind her a light bulb swayed on a wire, illuminating a stove and a few mattresses on the floor. In a tub, a zinc vat, crouched two children with foam in their hair, and she said hoarsely: 'Good evening! I would like to see Elisabeth.'

The music, the hubbub of voices and the clatter of plates and pots in the high-ceilinged stable swallowed her words. The woman she had spoken to held a hand behind her ear, and now Luisa recognized her: it was the milker with the painted fingernails. Her skin was slightly tanned, her wayward hair as black as her shaded eyes, she had a gently curving nose and beautiful slender lips which lent her features an elegant quality in spite of the apron that she wore, and when Luisa repeated herself more loudly, she replied: 'Then you've come to the right place. Come in, I have to wash the kids.'

The woman invited her in with a gesture – and Luisa's courage failed her. 'Thank you, many thanks, I don't want to bother you,' she said and smiled thinly. 'I just wanted to ask if you'd perhaps heard anything from your fiancé. We're friends, or rather acquaintances, he works for my father-in-law who owns the farm, and he gave me tips for my horse. It's getting much better already. So, I . . . we're getting worried, because he hasn't written yet, ever since he was called up. Not even to Herr Thamling, our administrator. Nobody knows how he is, whether he needs anything or what else is going on, and perhaps you have news of some kind? Is he wounded? Or well? Will he be coming back soon?'

The children giggled and splashed in the tub. The soapy water sloshed onto the floor, and she was already ashamed of herself for stammering – all the more so in that she thought she saw a hint of amusement, maybe even mockery, in the woman's expression. In spite of her youth she already had very fine spidery veins on her cheeks.

She took Luisa's wrist and pulled her over the threshold into the room. As she did so she looked at the little ones. 'What did I just say? Enough of this nonsense! Rinse your hair, wash your faces and then out of the tub! You'll be in bed in five minutes or you can forget about pudding!' She pulled a face and rolled her eyes to the beamed ceiling. 'My brothers,' she murmured. 'I've got another three like that, but thank God they can already wash themselves. If they wash at all.'

The room smelled of the hoof tar that had once been boiled up here, and she pointed to one of the stools by the table, took a box of Special Blend from her pocket and sat down opposite Luisa. There were sandy potatoes between them. 'So you know Walter? I bet he never mentioned me, the sly dog. Or maybe he did? Hang on a second . . . Are you the one from the big house, from the attic? The one with all the books?'

Luisa smiled, and the women tapped a half-smoked cigarette out of the pack. 'Oh, now I remember. You've got a big sister who's red-haired as well, isn't that right? A beautiful girl, she wears those elegant coats with the narrow waist and the Persian collar. And always stockings with seams and pointed shoes. She once came towards me arm in arm with an officer, and I stood there like a yokel in front of the Queen.'

She struck a match and dragged on the stump of her cigarette. 'I used to read too. I'd hide myself away with a big fat book for days on end. But now that my mother is ill all the time and I have to look after these little baggages, I never have the time.' Tilting her chin, she blew her smoke at the lamp. 'Walter's doing all right, I think. At least he writes like mad, you could paper walls with it. I would probably write back, but what is there to write about here? And also I have terrible handwriting, he wouldn't be able to decipher it . . . He's a driver down on Lake Balaton, in a supply unit, so some way from the firing. Do you want a glass of water? It's boiled.'

Luisa said no and studied the room. It had only one narrow window, a skylight; below it were three crooked metal cupboards, each with a padlock. The stone oven with the open chimney was black with tar, and the sink was chipped. There were no sheets on the straw sacks and mattresses along the wall, only horse blankets or plaids made of colourful patches, and in one corner there was a painting on the wall that she had often seen in every possible size in the Dreyer department store: a guardian angel behind two children on a rickety bridge.

'What's your favourite book?' the woman asked.

Luisa inflated her cheeks and thought. 'I don't know,' she said. 'It's constantly changing. I think *Winnetou I* is good, or *The Rider of the White Horse*, even though it was difficult. And I've read *Gone with the Wind* three times.'

The woman smiled broadly. Her teeth were straight but strangely grey, as if they were all filled with amalgam. 'Me too!' she said and threw a piece of wood in the stove. 'At least three times! When I was your age, twelve or so, I couldn't stop. In the library in Danzig they had two copies, one in German, one in English, and I kept extending my loan. And when that became impossible, I just borrowed the other one and had that loan extended too. After that both books were full of my notes.'

She sucked the air through the gaps in her teeth, rolled up one sleeve and scratched a series of flea bites until they turned red. 'But I never quite got to the end, I admit. It stopped being interesting when they had each other. And then Bonnie Blue is born, and gets a little horse, and then Bonnie Blue dies, and everyone becomes so . . .' She wrinkled her nose. 'No! I need crashes and bangs. When they were going at each other like knives, each of them cleverer than the other, and you didn't know if they were going to come together or not, I thought that was exciting. What about you?'

Luisa's elbow suddenly itched too. 'Well,' she said, 'it's dramatic all the way through and the ending's very sad as well. So, I cried quite a lot and eventually thought, that's enough, now they can live peacefully with their love. But then Rhett Butler is so bitter and cold, and Scarlett goes flying down the stairs . . .'

Naked and wet, one of the brothers pressed himself against Elisabeth, and she took a towel off the line that was stretched diagonally across the room. 'Oh you know, I was never as romantic as that. I always had too much scrubbing to do,' she murmured. 'And when you're tired you wouldn't care if the moon fell in your lap.'

With a cigarette in the corner of her mouth she dried the little boy and rubbed his hair, staring into the distance for a moment. 'Love, love, what is it after all?' The sound of bursting woodlice came from the stove, and then she blew the smoke out through her nostrils and said, 'We have to wait for love to come to us, don't we?'

The boy, with a thumb in his mouth, nodded dreamily, and Luisa asked, 'Why, though, what's up with Walter?'

Elisabeth shook her head. 'Hm, who knows what'll come of all that. We hadn't known each other very long. But it's true, he's quite the vision. Those eyes, those muscles, and when he laughs the sun comes out . . . Right after the first kiss I wanted to have children with him, a whole stable full of them. I mean, it's idiotic, isn't it? I'm breaking my back here sorting out my brothers, not to mention Mum with her thyroid, and on top of that I want to have brats with a complete stranger? It was a fever or something like it.'

She got to her feet and hung the towel over the line again. As she did so she noticed Luisa's eyes on her boots, which were old and fragile where they kinked; the linen fabric could be seen behind the rubber. 'Nifty bit of foot-wear, don't you think? I've worn better,' she said. 'But we were in the field when the Russians came. They shot Grandpa straight away, right in front of our eyes. Just because he was a man. He fell in the ditch like a plank of wood, and we weren't even allowed to go back to the farmhouse. We were chased to the four winds, in rubber boots. We didn't meet up again until we got to Konitz.'

She flicked the butt of her cigarette at the hole in the oven, but missed it. It fell on the floor, and the bigger of the boys, in pyjamas now, picked it up and sucked on it greedily, holding his naked brother away from him with an outstretched arm. Their sister turned around, gave both of them a slap and pointed to the beds, and it was only now that Luisa noticed how big this delicate woman's hands were, and how callused. She edged closer to the table and asked under her breath: 'Were you raped?'

Elisabeth didn't visibly give a start; she just closed her eyes briefly, and something grey darted across her face, the shadow of a far-off insult. 'Heavens, child, the questions you ask,' she murmured and took a knife from the drawer, whetted it on the sink and took a big potato from the pile. Her eyelids, also full of delicate veins, twitched constantly as if something had got inside them. And yet she wielded the blade so carefully – it was visible through the peel.

'Yes,' she said at last and took a deep breath, 'one of them got me in some godforsaken . . . I had been walking for hours, I was thirsty and I thought the farmhouse was empty. Two dogs lay dead in the garden. And then I go into the kitchen and he's sitting right behind the door and he bangs it closed quicker than I can get out. So I was in a trap. Since then the smell of schnapps has always made me throw up.' She raised her head and blew a few stray hairs out of her forehead. 'So? Anything else you want to know?'

It sounded sharp and sarcastic, and was at any rate meant to be conclusive. She went on slowly peeling. But

Luisa, after glancing at the children, who were playing with cork cars, hooked her fingers under the table and asked quietly, almost in a whisper: 'Did it hurt a lot?'

The peel, the long spiral, broke, and one corner of Elisabeth's mouth turned down. There was a dark gravity in her eyes, and although she was swallowing her voice was thick. 'Goodness, what a darling you are,' she said. 'What do you think? That he sang me poems by Pushkin? Not everyone's as lucky as Scarlett O'Hara!' With her painted thumbnail she scratched an eye out of the potato and threw it in the sink. 'But, well, forget it. Presumably the poor bastard's already dead too. The main thing is, I didn't get knocked up.'

The sudden shame at awakening these memories made Luisa turn red; she could see it in the little mirror above the tap. There was a crack in the glass, duplicating her features, which struck her as strangely unfamiliar with their black rims and painted lashes, as if someone else were looking at her, and she got to her feet and buttoned up her coat. Elisabeth was startled. 'Oh, what? You're not going already? Really? That's a shame! When we were making friends so nicely . . .'

The girl mentioned the evening milking, and the woman wiped her eyes dry with the balls of her hands. 'Well all right then,' she said, 'I'm sure we'll see each other again. They don't know what to do with us. We're as welcome here as the plague. "The refugees grow fat each day and take our feather beds away!" it said in a pub in Tarp yesterday, written up in chalk. If I write back to Walter I'll send him your regards, regards from the little redhead with the reading habit, OK?'

Then she got up, walked to the stove and hung the potato peel over the line to dry; ground up, it could be used as starch. 'By the way: in your farmhouse over there, is there actually a bathtub? A proper big one, not just a children's bowl?'

Luisa said yes, and Elisabeth opened the door to her. Something shy flickered in her eyes, which made her look more delicate, girlish, and in a low voice she added: 'I don't want to be a nuisance, but do you think I could come to yours to wash? Just for an hour? I haven't lain in a proper tub with hot water for ages. Of course I'll bring firewood.'

A sad tune was being played on the accordion, a woman sang in a high voice; Luisa pulled on her gloves. Once again she looked at the other woman's rotten boots, and her desire to help ran up against the idea of her mother, who hadn't liked refugees even in Kiel, not even as cleaners in the flat, because they supposedly brought in illnesses and stole. And she shrugged and said, 'I think so. I'll ask.'

The times grew harder, and they who thought they had nothing left to lose, while famine persisted and pestilence laid people in the earth, lost even more. The author of these lines had barely the strength to continue with his chronicle of woe, as ailing physics stirred his medicine. But the misty phantom of his vision floated always before him, the little flame above the water: it was his ideal. The chapel, God help every last one of us, belonged in the village, and as wise Euripides has it: many obstacles – many ways. Because anyone who believes that a dream can be buried, let him slip into the bower of night and steal the shoes of sleep!

Since the effort to win the carpenter Johann Bubenleb for the plan had foundered on his reluctance, it would have been apt to seek enthusiasm elsewhere, a sturdy young man who knew how to swing an axe in return for a strong drink. Meanwhile a sacred task had to be performed by someone with not only strength but also skill, which is not to be disdained. In fact it needs a clear mind, in which the work is determined before the first blow, indeed before the existence of the nail, still glowing as ore in the seam. Whereby it is relatively unimportant whether the man is too old or too weak to brace a beam. God forgives the pious bricklayer a crooked wall.

In the weary eyes of the goatherd Johann Bubenleb, now, wrapped in his cloud of pipe smoke, the writer had seen this spirit. Slumbering within it was a promise; he knocked on the goatherd's door to reawaken it, and the man let him in, offered him a chair and said, not without a chuckle: Bredelin, old Merxheim! Your stubbornness is strange at a time when the earth is full to the brim with armies raging furiously with one another and appealing to God and dedicating their burning banners to the Devil. It is hard to imagine anyone today doing anything without a desire for bread or self-advancement, particularly bringing things into order. What good, he asked frankly, was a prayer-house in the village, when all had ceased to pray?

The pipe crackled, the goats tugged gently on the sackcloth which poverty had declared should be his garb, and the chidden fellow sighed with care: you are probably right, Master Bubenleb, forgive a dreamer his dream, but the idea had come to me that a man should do something that gives his earthly span a value for ever. Something that might be nothing to other human beings, but everything to God. To put it another way: what use are books in times when no one reads? They are dead paper, nothing more. And yet they keep the mystery alive.

The old man shook his head. You have something about you of the hidden priest, he murmured, and his voice sounded dark with smoke: fever or hunger have given you a picture in your head, you posturing penman, to which lunacy has added colour. A chapel is not a ship, or only in your drunken verses, a chapel cannot swim. It will drown and sink to the bottom of the lake, a home for fishes and the bones of the dead. And the bell will decay into rust.

Then let it be so! the writer pursued more urgently, inspired by the dispute: but what is a ship? Heavy wood, as hard as rock, cast iron, a hold full of bullets, cattle and cannon, not counting the people. And yet, what a miracle, it shoots across the waves like an arrow. And does it know why? Not because it has sails and is saved by the wind from sinking, rather because it glides upon the mercy of the Lord! But what about a house that is erected in His honour? Do we not speak of the church as a vessel?

Bredelin! the master roared and snuffed the wick: he speaks as if piss were flowing through his brain – a ship floats because its shape, according to the bow, the hull, the curve of the cheeks, repels the water, like the wooden bowl of eggs that the maid puts in the tub to cool. Or indeed: the greater the immersive depth because of its freight, taking the height of the walls into consideration, the stronger the pressure of the waves against it, and the uplift makes it float. That is the principle of Archimedes, not the mercy of anyone! Let him read the masters of science rather than pious mumbo-jumbo!

Puffing, he lit his pipe again, and the writer kneaded his dappled fingers and appeared appropriately contrite. The years remaining to me are not mine, he replied, and perhaps the ink in my quill is already running low. Because if I understand you correctly, good man, and I am sure that I do not, a chapel, and a small one to boot, a bit of plaster, beams and whitewash, cannot in fact be too heavy, can it?

Then seen in the light of Archimedes, correct me, only the right vessel, equipped with hull and bow and curving cheeks, is all that is needed to bring it to our shores? Humbly the writer lowered his head, but blinked up at an angle and added more quietly: and did Master Bubenleb not also study shipbuilding?

Then the man, the light of destiny in his old eyes, was struck by so great a dream. He stroked his animals' beards and viewed his rusty tools, the square, the dividers and the saws on the wall. Even though he was weary from the years that had taken it out of him, he was a seasoned craftsman of curses and stinking farts, he had been cheated of his livelihood – he is no raw apprentice. Rather he is one of those who know of the secret that dwells in wood as it does in hair, and had woken with headaches before all the stars had risen in the night.

Damn it all, Merxheim, he croaked, your ravings are as tough as wood shavings. And as dry! Then he pulled a hidden bottle from the fireplace and filled the earthen beakers with a red wine that had matured before the hard times and lent the plans, drawn with a flying hand, a decent glow. Cheese and bread appeared too, and one song succeeded another. By the end the candles had almost burnt down, it was in good spirits the writer walked through thick smoke to the door, and when he drunkenly reached for the latch, filled with confidence and good wine, his hand gripped the horn of a friendly goat.

Dusk was already falling when Luisa took her seat behind her parents in the car, the battered VW utility vehicle. The rock-crystal keyring rocked back and forth, and they argued loudly and ignored their daughter, which was a relief to her. Bent over the book that Frau Thamling had left on her stairs, poems by Andreas Gryphius, she tried to read the Gothic script in the fading light.

Not only had she painted her eyelashes and emphasized her cheekbones with rouge, her lips were also made up for the first time. The make-up was slightly taut on her skin, and she kept having to remind herself not to run the tip of her tongue over it to get rid of the lardy taste. It even made her feel slightly ill, as the smell of cod-liver oil had once made her do; yet she had liked the dark red in the mirror.

When her mother shook her head, the long feathers from her hat scraped the fabric cover of the roof. Her eyes grew moist. 'I'm not blind,' she said. 'I know exactly what your type is! Your gold teeth haven't flashed like that in ages. You're getting worse and worse, I don't want to know what goes on in my absence in Kiel. All it takes is for some young gypsy thing to come and flash her eyes at you, and you immediately lose all self-control!'

Luisa's father fiddled nervously with the ignition key, and the headlights went on and off several times. 'That's enough now,' he said. 'It was a professional conversation, and it'll be useful to you too. I wanted something from her, and just because I'm being kind to a woman it certainly doesn't mean I'm being unfaithful. That's how cultivated people behave, you know.' He looked at his watch with a sigh. 'Where's our film star got to, damn it? I don't want to drive in the dark again.'

'Cultivated people!' Luisa's mother sneered; her voice was quivering. 'You should have seen yourself! A paunchy, balding old goat! I can vividly imagine what you wanted from her. And you probably got it, too. In fact I'm sure of it.' She took out one of her crocheted handkerchiefs and dabbed her eyes. 'What, excuse me, is cultivated about stealing your own wife's shoes and giving them to a complete stranger? You couldn't have demonstrated your contempt of me more clearly. I hate you, you . . . Why did I ever drag you out of that gas oven?'

Luisa's father turned up the collar of his coat and breathed on his hands. 'My God, because you love me,' he murmured, and it sounded weary, almost resigned. 'If you could only hear yourself! How could I take your shoes from you? I don't even know where you keep them! And as regards your suspicions: I talked to the young woman about a job, nothing else, Gerda. The British are advancing, and soon I'm going to need waitresses who can speak English. That little girl has been to middle school, she's hard working and quick, and she's also served in party tents, in Danzig or somewhere.' He impatiently struck the horn. 'Ask your daughter!'

Luisa looked up, cleared her throat and said, 'Yes, that's right. She's the one you wouldn't allow to have a bath at our house. She's read *Gone with the Wind* in the original and looks after her brothers and her sick mother. Her boyfriend, one of the milkers here, is very nice.' Even though it had been too dark for some time to make out anything on the pages, she flicked through the book, which smelled slightly of basement, and wrapped the ribbon around her finger. 'Oh and by the way, I gave her the shoes.'

Her father looked at her quickly out of the corner of his eye and raised an eyebrow, a silent Oh my! Her mother turned around. Her mouth was crooked, her expression thunderstruck. 'You did what?' she hissed. 'You? You're not serious, are you?' Watery mascara ran down her cheek, a grey streak. 'Why would you do something like that, child? Have you lost your mind?'

Luisa swallowed and looked out of the window. Herr Thamling was leading a horse past, and a loose horseshoe clattered on the road. 'Well, she needed a pair,' she said in a low voice. 'They were too small for you, too unmodern for Billie and too big for me. The poor girl had only rubber boots, completely ruined from her flight, so I thought we could help. They suit her, don't they?'

Her mother crumpled the handkerchief until it had disappeared completely in her fist, and glared at her: 'I'm about to fly off the handle. You can't just give away my . . . Those are classic college shoes, frame-stitched! What do you imagine Gudrun paid for them, with the leather shortage? They're made to measure, I had to give them a plaster-cast in Lübeck! They have natural rubber soles and real silver buckles – and that Pole woman wears them to go milking in the byre? Oh my God, what kind of spawn have I brought into the world!'

She shook her head in disbelief; a tear dripped from her chin. 'You know what I think, Luisa? You know what's becoming increasingly clear to me, seriously now? Your interminable books are turning your head. That frivolous nonsense is driving you completely mad, it certainly is! No normal person would do such a thing!'

She had spat these words through gritted teeth, gripping her handkerchief as if she wanted to tear off its crocheted corners. Her husband rested a hand on her arm. 'Come on, Gerda, calm down now,' he said. 'It's not the end of the world, is it? Take a deep breath and be honest: you waddled rather than walked in those orthopaedic boots. You have much nicer shoes, and more comfortable ones too. Think of your fat feet.'

His wife sniffed. 'Of course, I'm not surprised at all,' she said, 'that you should stand up for her . . . You two are cut from the same cloth. If you think about it, I have no one in the world, not a soul, only my Gudrun. And she hasn't visited me for days. She probably won't even call in on me once she has her child! Oh goodness, what's the point. What I'd really like to do is go away for ever, away from the lot of you. But then who will take me in . . .'

She drew in her lips and whimpered quietly, and Luisa reached between the seats and stroked her hand, gripped her fingers. There was a gold ring on almost every one.

'He's right, though, Mummy dearest. Those shoes didn't suit you at all. They were much too flat, and those Mozart buckles made you look older than you are. You looked like a grandma in them.'

Her mother gave a barely perceptible start. Her eyes closed, her eyelids wrinkled as if she were in pain, she repeatedly shook her head, the longest feather, a curved one from a golden pheasant, scratching the fabric roofliner a little later than the others.

'You think so?' she sighed at last and stared into the park. Mist rose from the river and drifted through the open tea-house, and the faun on his mossy plinth seemed to float. 'That's even possible, isn't it? I always suspected that, in front of the mirror, I mean. You always immediately look squat on low heels, and less graceful too. Basically I'm more of a wedge type. They have these light cork soles now . . .'

Then she gulped back her tears once and for all, took out her little make-up tin and said in her usual voice, a little hoarse from smoking. 'And now fetch your sister, please! We always have to wait for the child.'

*

The drive to Osterrönfeld near Rendsburg, where Vinzent and Gudrun lived, usually took less than twenty minutes. But as the darkness deepened Luisa's father had to drive more slowly; the light that forced its way through the slits in the rubber hoods was barely enough to see a few paces ahead. Every now and again a kilometre stone was chalked by the side of the road, and the herd of deer running across the road in front of them could only be made out by the paler escutcheons on their hind-quarters.

Deep purple the last strip of daylight over the fields. Luisa surreptitiously studied her sister's silhouette. Her coat was open, and she was wearing the white dress with the ruched neckline and the gold brooch between her breasts. She had smoothed her curls, a slightly darker red than Luisa's own, and rolled them vertically at the back of her head as Gudrun had done. Together with her straight nose and slightly curved lips that looked very elegant – but also rather odd, because her hair had never been so thick. 'What have you got under there?' Luisa asked and reached out an arm to touch the structure. Billie immediately twisted her head to the side. 'Hands off!' she hissed. 'Mind your own business!'

She raised a menacing elbow, and her mother said: 'She's stuck Aunt Tilli's lovely red velvet pincushion in there. Without asking me, of course . . . By the way, I'd like to see it again, young lady!' Then she nudged her husband and pointed to the road, the shiny cobbles. 'Look out, Wilhelm, there's something ahead.'

*

A torch was being swung in a high arc. Luisa's father braked the car, which skidded slightly in the evening dew, and opened the side window. In the darkness there was a rhythmical stamping and clattering that sounded like a mill wheel or a wooden machine, and a soldier in an oilskin cape directed the torch at their number plate. Then he lit them individually, studying Billie for a little longer than the others, then turned the torch off again and shouted: 'Stick to the extreme right. And keep your windows closed.'

Luisa's father accelerated cautiously, and they drove slowly past a row of dark-clad people. No faces could be seen, only sometimes a flash of wide-open eyes, white teeth in a distorted mouth, with a cloud of icy breath in front of it. The wheezing of the marching men sounded as if they were counting their steps, and only the well-fed armed men walking beside them made it clear how thin the figures in the wooden shoes really were.

Picks and shovels they carried over their shoulders, and visibly heavy bags, and suddenly Luisa recognized the smell, the aroma of sour earth in the moor, and whispered: 'They're convicts. They live in the camp in the Klosterwald.'

A whipcrack rang out; her father closed the window and shifted up a gear. 'No,' he said, 'that's not right, darling. Convicts are criminals, and most of these people aren't. They were arrested without being tried or sentenced, they were simply locked up because somebody didn't like their way of thinking or the look of their face. So they're prisoners but not convicts, do you see that? It's a difference that probably doesn't matter much to them in their situation. But if there's nothing we can do for them, we should at least give them that respect.'

Brightly the moon rose behind them, the canal water was white, and his wife clicked her tongue irritably. 'Good Lord, the things you come out with! What's the point of this pedantry? As if the child wasn't disturbed enough.' Then she turned around and said, 'And you will please keep away from the Klosterwald, it's forbidden to all of us! I don't want to find myself at the police station on your account! They'll lock me up too in the end!'

Luisa nodded. The huge railway bridge that passed high above the canal, with its twisting approaches, came into view. Fixed to the pylon on the Rendsburg side were circling spotlights, anti-aircraft guns were mounted on the pylon on the near side, and soldiers were walking about on the landing stages. The ferry glided across the water on long wire cables, women and children sat scaling fish on the shore along the Krähenberg, and Sibylle, straightening her neckline and patting her hair, asked: 'What do you think? Will the Grand Admiral be there today?'

Her mother buttoned up her coat. 'He announced as much,' she said. 'But who knows these days. I'd rather not think about all the things such a man would have to deal with. Vinzent said recently that if the Führer goes to Linz, to his retirement home, Dönitz will be the first candidate for his successor. And he would make quite an impression with his straight posture and his clear gaze. At least in the photographs you can see that he always stands at the front on the navigation bridge and . . .' She took a breath, a startled yap. 'My God, it occurs to me: how do you address a Grand Admiral? Do you simply shake hands?'

She looked at her husband, who shook his head slowly and turned into the avenue of plane trees in front of the old semi-circular house. 'Well, that depends on your sex,' he said, putting his foot on the brake. 'So for example I always curtsy . . .'

*

They could already hear music. The high windows of the villa were in darkness, but on the steps candles flickered in glass vases. Above the main door, on garlands of yew branches, a silver-plated '40' swayed in the wind. The limousines and staff cars in the forecourt, many with SS runes on their number plates, two even bearing standards, parked beneath a stretched net. The moon cast shadows from the rubber leaves on it, and chauffeurs sat behind some of the windows. 'Just take a look at that,' Luisa's father murmured as he parked the car next to the others. 'All Reich limos and security service. I'd recommend the Hitler salute, but also the "German glance". I'm not staying long, I can tell you that straight away. I'm off to Kiel first thing tomorrow.'

'Why?' Billie said, dabbing a drop of perfume behind her ear and snapping shut her flat handbag, which was covered entirely with pearls. 'Aren't they your customers? You live off them.'

Her father, who had smoothed his eyebrows with damp fingertips, got out of the car. 'We all live off them,' he said and looked at her new dress. 'And it's not a bad living either. But that's not to say by any means that I have to like them.' He reached under his lapel and pinned his Party badge on the outside. 'Is my tie straight?'

The drive was lined by a hedge of low boxwood balls. Luisa could feel the sharp gravel on the courtyard through the soles of her ballet shoes, but when she trod on the old steps leading up to the front door, the weathered sandstone, a pleasing shiver ran through her as always. 'What's the German glance?' she asked, and operated the door knocker, a heavy ring with a crow's head.

The beak pecked against the brass shield, and her father replied under his breath: 'Always look over your shoulder before you say anything. You never know who might be standing behind you taking notes!'

A young waitress, with a blonde braid wrapped around her head in a crown, opened the door to them. Several uniformed men and their wives were standing in the panelled foyer with the curved oak stairs and the huge painting of a wheat field. The family handed in their coats at the cloakroom counter, and when Luisa saw her face under the sparkling lights in the mirror she gave a start. Everything was overdrawn and too thickly applied under the dim light bulbs in the attic, and she quickly turned away from the others and took a handkerchief out of her sleeve. Her lipstick was stubborn, and it smeared; for a moment she looked as if she'd been binging on strawberry jam.

Vinzent and Gudrun received their guests beneath the stucco arch of the drawing-room door and she let some saliva drip onto the cotton fabric and also rubbed the rouge from her cheeks as best she could. She thought no one had noticed, since she was standing both behind a grandfather clock and behind her parents, who were waiting to hand their present over to their son-in-law; her father was holding a forty-year-old bottle of Armagnac in a cedar case. But Gudrun, who had had her hair done in an Olympic roll and was wearing a floor-length pink dress with a bow under the bosom, which was supposed to accentuate her belly, saw it none the less. She pressed her fists against her hips and shouted past all the birthday guests: 'Dear God, can it be? Are you wearing make-up? Who did that to you?'

Two officers turned towards Luisa, and only now did her parents notice. With her cream-coloured organza stole on her elbows, her mother sucked a corner of her mouth into her cheek and shook her head with a quiet grunt as if she had just witnessed some sort of childish behaviour, while the silent admiration of her father, emphasized by his raised brows, exuded a melancholy that made Luisa's eyes glisten, for whatever reason. She wanted to comfort him and didn't know where to look, and when she quietly wished her brother-in-law a happy birthday with her arm outstretched, she actually curtsied out of embarrassment.

Her cheeks burned, but Vinzent, in a black dinner jacket with gleaming silk lapels, drew her to him and said between his teeth: 'Let them talk. You're allowed to emphasize what you've got, aren't you? Your beauty will be a present to me this evening.' Again he ran his thumb across the palm of her hand as if to rub away the sweat there. 'I'll show you the new bunker later.'

There was gentle mockery in Sibylle's smile, but she offered her elbow, and with relief Luisa linked arms and stepped with her into the big drawing room. Black SS and red swastika flags hung on the walls of the oval room, which was crowned by an acanthus frieze and already very full. Officers' caps lay on almost all of the sideboards and window seats, some with silver braids or death's heads above the brim, and the fingers of pastel-coloured gloves protruded from the ladies' handbags behind them.

The chairs and sofas had been pushed up against the walls, and people were chatting in small groups. Many women wore evening gowns with tight bodices and wide puffy skirts, and strapped pumps or dancing shoes of patent leather, satin or velvet, whose manufacture had been prohibited long since. There were also traditional costumes from the various Gau areas, and Husum lace caps, and Billie, who was wearing gold stud earrings, straightened her collar and said, 'Stockings, skirt and dark-blue wool jacket with a white blouse, it looks good. But I'd actually leave out the rouge, little one; it stands out too obviously against your pale skin. And your mouth is still too fresh for lipstick. On the other hand always paint your eyelashes twice, trust me. Otherwise we redheads look as if we haven't got any eyelashes at all.'

A uniformed man at a grand piano with the word 'Bösendorfer' on it was playing operetta tunes, and a waiter in tails held out a tray of glasses of sparkling wine. Billie wedged her envelope bag under her armpit, picked up the fullest glass and half-drained it with a gulp. But Luisa declined, she hadn't been feeling well since the morning. 'And what about perfume?' she asked, sniffing her shoulder. 'How much are you supposed to use? One drop? Two?'

'Oh, that's not so simple,' her sister said. 'You can easily overdo it. The best thing to do is get hold of a bottle with a pump, spray a quick burst in the air and walk through the cloud. That's the most elegant way. What you smell here, by the way, is gardenia, freshly arrived from France and impossibly expensive. If you steal so much as a sniff of it, I'll scatter your books with rat poison!'

Then she drained the rest of her glass and watched a tall civilian with a pearl on his tie as he passed in front of her. 'That plonk's not too bad,' she said, smacking her lips. 'It could even be champagne. But right now I'd rather have a tasty man. I haven't danced for an eternity.'

As they walked among the people, many women looked askance at Sibylle, and she smiled at an officer, probably an acquaintance, standing at the 'harbour bar' set up specially for the party and decorated with nets and pennants. But no sooner had he made his cheek bulge with his tongue than Sibylle seemed to see straight through him, and when Luisa asked her if the Grand Admiral had arrived she jutted her chin. 'Very unlikely,' she murmured. 'Not a halo to be seen. Perhaps he's standing at the buffet and gobbling down all our Russian caviar.'

The pianist interrupted his playing with a flourish at the keyboard, and a white-haired woman, plumper than the people one generally saw during those years, approached the grand piano. Many guests surrounded the pedestal as she unfolded a sheet of paper, a densely typed page, and Billie let out a low moan. She pushed with her shoulder against a mirrored door, tugged on Luisa's woollen jacket, and stole with her into the adjacent dining room. 'Honoured guests, my dear Vini . . .'

Lamps made of antlers hung on the walls, which were lined with dark red leather. Bar tables with white cloths had been set up, and in an old glass cabinet, alongside all kinds of Meissen figurines, a service was displayed in such a way that the gold swastikas were visible on the base of the mocha cups.

Behind a long buffet, between columns of plates and bowls, staff stood in naval blouses, waiting to be able to serve the guests their starters: smoked eel, marinated roast beef, pumpernickel with shrimps and dill. There were potato, pasta and spinach salads, half-eggs with sardines, stuffed cucumbers, Bismarck herrings and salmon tartare. In the middle of the table, still with the bristles on its hoof, lay a wild boar ham, and behind it the main courses steamed, a row of rectangular pans heated by little paraffin flames, full of mashed potato, rice with peas, sole and bacon and all kinds of sliced roast meats. The whole thing was crowned by a many-layered marzipan cake with a chocolate '40' at the end of the buffet, where candlelight shone through jelly and candied fruits.

Flickering in the draught, it was reflected in the rimless glasses of a man handing out plates from a stack. He wore a dark flannel suit with waistcoat and watch chain, and had a whitish duelling scar below his cheekbone, proud flesh. 'Yes, amazing, isn't it? It's almost incredible,' he said, and smiled at the wondering girls, who were slightly at a loss in the face of such variety. 'In Berlin they're eating the mildew from the basement walls, and here . . . How many warehouses do you think were looted for this?'

His hair, combed straight back, smelled of birch water, and ignoring the staff he took a chicken leg from the buffet and added in an undertone: 'Children, enjoy this war, the peace is going to be terrible!'

Then he looked at Sibylle, her high breasts, and whispered something in her ear that made her laugh, embarrassed and mocking at the same time. When she turned away from him with a shake of the head, her underpinned hairdo swayed slightly, and the man, with a gilt-edged Party badge on his jacket, also nodded to Luisa. 'I was just telling your sister that she looks like that Queen of Egypt, the beautiful one,' he said, smiling with plainly false teeth and biting off a mouthful of meat. 'But I couldn't remember the name. You're sisters, aren't you? What's your name?'

Luisa asked for a lemon tart. Colourful hundreds and thousands trickled from it and crunched under their shoes. 'Nefertiti,' she murmured distractedly, left Billie alone with the man and stepped into the little bay window, enclosed in velvet curtains, at the end of the room. In that corner, which held a library from Gudrun's time as a teacher, there was a chaise longue next to a palm tree, and she lifted the blackout blind high enough to see the glittering Kaiser Wilhelm Canal, over a hundred metres wide at that spot.

The transporter bridge swung over from Rendsburg before disappearing behind a row of silos, and she drew her feet up onto the cushion and spooned the cream from the pastry. After the speech in the drawing room, after the cheers and applause, music was played again, a record this time, Marika Rökk. Luisa knew the voice from the radio and moved her head back and forth. In the next room people were starting to dance, although she couldn't see them since the door to the drawing room was only slightly open; but after only a few bars the steps of many pairs of dancers set the old parquet floor vibrating and the tips of the palms twitched. '*In der Nacht ist der Mensch nicht gerne alleine* – No one likes to be alone at night.'

They sang along with those lines. Outside the stars dimmed in the light of the circling anti-aircraft lights, dimmed and then flashed again. A completely dark navy ship, a massive tower of steel and shadow and dull grey, from which the gun barrels pointed in all directions, glided slowly past the house towards the Baltic, towards Kiel harbour. No one could be seen on deck or behind the black windows and portholes, and the water only wrinkled a little in front of the pointed bow. At one point on the ruptured starboard side the ribs were exposed, inadequately concealing the huge banner fastened to the railing and the anchors with the inscription 'The Jews wanted this war!'

*

She lowered the blind again, switched on the reading lamp and flicked through a picture book. It was a book of photographs from Africa: men with painted bodies and spears in the savannah, women with pointed breasts skinning an antelope, children wrestling by a fire with meat roasting on it. The paws of a sleeping cheetah hung from a treetop, and a black marabou stork prowled like an inspector through the shallow water otherwise occupied only by flamingos.

Luisa gave a start. The people at the buffet also interrupted their chat to see where the scream had come from. Throwing her sequined dress and petticoats around her like foam, so that her stocking tops could be seen, a woman rushed from the room, skidded by the balcony door and reached for the handle. Her smile was radiant, the glance with which she looked back over her shoulder before disappearing into the night was filled with wild awe, and the guests at the standing tables, spoons or forks raised halfway to their mouths, turned their heads curiously.

But the gaunt officer in the gala uniform who followed

her a few heartbeats later was in no hurry. Striding at a moderate pace he greeted the assembled party, a brief nod with his chin raised, once rested his fingertips on his temple, and only revealed the true urgency of his situation by making the mistake of closing the door before he was fully standing on the terrace. The tip of his dagger of honour in its silver-plated sheath was still sticking into the room, and the clatter made everybody jump.

'Ah, this spring,' Gudrun said, suddenly standing by the bay window. The ribbon on her pink dress was orange, as were her shiny satin shoes, and she folded her fingers over her belly and smiled at her stepsister. 'Men are children, aren't they? They always want to play chasey. But why are you sitting here on your own like this? Don't you like it at our house?'

'I do,' Luisa said politely and smoothed her skirt. 'It's lovely, it's very festive, thank you. I'd just like to read for a while.'

Gudrun touched the curls above her ear, rolled into the shape of a snail, and looked at her with a frown. 'At my party? Hm, I don't know . . . Are you really reading? Or are you just hiding behind your books so that you don't have to talk to anyone and can pursue your own dreams? Come, child, mingle with the people a little, we've got interesting guests. They'll teach you how the world really works.'

She stepped beneath the fringed pelmet and looked at the book along with her: the sun was falling beyond the river on whose shores the buffaloes and zebras drank, and here and there the eyes of crocodiles flashed in the murky water. 'Yes, I'll do it in a minute,' Luisa said. 'I've been wondering that too. But right now I've got a bit of a headache.'

With a sigh Gudrun pointed to the windowsill, to the plate with the unfinished cake. 'Then perhaps you should get something proper to eat, don't you think? Potatoes, roast meat or eel, so that you put on a bit of weight. I've been wondering for some time why you don't gain anything on the farm, where there's any amount of fat. And incidentally men don't like bean-poles, you know. If they grab you as they do it's always better to have a bit of upholstery.' She smiled. 'But yes, perhaps it's a bit early to think about such things . . . Or am I mistaken, does the make-up have a deeper meaning? Are you finally trying to catch up with Billie?'

Without looking up, Luisa shook her head and went on flicking the pages. One chimpanzee with a silver-grey furry back was sniffing the growth-like hindquarters of another, and she wrinkled her nose and said, 'No, I'm not doing that.'

Gudrun sat down beside her and ran the back of her fingers over Luisa's cheek. Her wedding ring felt cool. 'And I have no idea what's supposed to be pretty about it. The natural look is still the best one for us. And you shouldn't pay any attention to her opinions, believe me. That sort of loose talk could cost you your life. You've heard the way she used to talk about the Führer and his victory. What on earth put such crazy thoughts in her head? That fashion-obsessed girl hasn't got a clue about politics. And tell me, is it true about Dad, and his endless drunken chatter?'

Luisa frowned. 'What do you mean?' she asked hoarsely. 'I don't remember. Did you just break wind?'

'Excuse me?' Gudrun, startled, leapt to her feet. 'Oh God, that's quite possible, sorry!' she whispered and opened a window. 'That darned brat is so impetuous already, it's unbelievable. That fluttering feeling was quite pleasant at first, but recently it's been trampling on my guts every minute of the day. Perhaps it really will be a boy.' She flapped her hand through the air and gave a pained smile. 'Is that better?'

Luisa shrugged. 'It didn't bother me. By the way, do you know that in horse-breeding you can tell the sex of the unborn animal very easily? For example if a mare has a female foal in her belly, she stands calmly and peacefully among the others in the pasture and eats grass. But if she's pregnant with a stallion she gets irritable and aggressive and keeps mounting other mares, as if she were a stallion herself. Incredible, isn't it?'

Gudrun laughed, but it sounded wooden. 'My God, what a crazy thing you are,' she said and closed the window. As she did so she studied her stepsister with the appraising seriousness of a teacher who can't tell whether a child is naive or unusually refined. 'Is that really true?' she asked. 'Or is it just another thing you made up?'

Herr Thamling had told her, but before she could say so, Vinzent joined them, holding a glass in front of his smiling mouth. 'So this is the cave where the most beautiful girls of the evening are hiding,' he said and put his arm around his wife. 'While I'm getting bored to death with those wizened and bemedalled old raisins out there, you're telling each other the wildest love stories, isn't that right? I can hear you!'

His pointed lapels stuck out over the chest of his dinner jacket, and Gudrun smiled up at him. 'You're not the only one with secrets, my friend . . . I've just been given a lesson in poetic biology, very interesting. And I'm trying to persuade our little one here that it would be a good idea for her to mingle with the people. She doesn't need to be quite as forward as her sister, who's letting them write their addresses on her stocking. But I'm sure that a bit of conversation with such a cultivated girl would delight our guests.' She straightened his bow tie. 'But she seems to prefer the society of books.'

Vinzent took a sip and smacked his lips. 'Which I understand very well!' he replied. 'Before my life with you I had the happiest hours of my life in the old agricultural college in Malente, in the library. Those comfortable armchairs with the foot supports, that incredible peace! You could spend whole afternoons dozing among the shelves.' He winked at Luisa, set the glass down and hugged Gudrun more tightly. 'Will you come then, please? Duty calls; Hinrich has already asked for you twice. He probably needs another speech . . .'

*

Applause rang out, and the slender exultation of a cornet. The piano and a bass joined in, and suddenly the door at the back end of the dining room was thrown open. Brightly coloured paper streamers shot through the air and hung on the antler lamps, and amidst loud singing a conga came

144

stamping past the buffet; the lined-up glasses tinkled against one another. The glittering lights on the sauces trembled, cherries rolled from the jellies, and cream toppings sank in on themselves as the horrified staff tried to wave away the confetti snowing down on them with napkins or their bare hands. 'As fast as the propeller spins, the pilot's wanton joy begins . . .'

Sibylle was in the line as well, smiling broadly, and she nodded to Luisa to join in. It was her lovely, free, slightly frivolous smile; it seemed to create a glittering space around her. But Luisa just waved and stayed sitting where she was with her book, and when her sister disappeared through the drawing-room door with the others she could see a strand of hair slipping on the back of her head, revealing the red velvet pincushion. 'Pilot, greet the sky for me / give my love to the Milky Way / across the vault of heaven you speed / until the break of day!'

*

The song grew quieter. For a moment the smell of sweat and perfume overwhelmed the aroma of the food, and an old waiter in tails that were far too big for him picked up things that the partygoers had lost: a cufflink, hairpins, a pair of glasses.

Raising the hem of her coffee-coloured brocade dress slightly, Luisa's mother stepped through the French windows and watched after the conga line. She had put the stole, which was really supposed to cover her upper arms, around her neck like a scarf, and stood sighing by the bay window. 'The wind is mild, everything smells of spring and the sea, and the bridge and the roofs are intact, as they were in peacetime. The residents of Rendsburg must be good people. Have you seen my daughter?'

Luisa giggled quietly and turned the pages. Elephants trotted through the savannah in a cloud of dust, the young among the legs of the adults. 'Mum, I am your daughter . . .'

She waved a hand dismissively and looked at the sweets on the buffet. 'Of course, child, I know. You're my darling, you always will be. Right now I mean the other one, our Gudrun. She's behaving so strangely, don't you think? She was going to get me some drops for my heart and that nail-fungus tincture, and she hasn't said a word about it, just imagine. I think she's cutting me out. She's staying out of my way, God alone knows why.'

She chose a bowl of redcurrant pudding with vanilla sauce. 'And did you hear Vinzent's mother's speech? All that boasting about his talents and connections? No? Reich Marshal and Grand Admiral here, Magda Goebbels there, but not a word about our family, not one! We don't even exist as far as she's concerned! When I congratulated her on her son earlier on and said our Gudrun might have come from modest circumstances but was always in good health, I just meant that she didn't need to worry about her grandchild. Always in tip-top condition, not even measles! "She won't cost you a penny," I said, obviously joking. And she looks at me as if I'd pooped on her shoes. Where is your father?'

Luisa shrugged and turned the page. A flock of tiny birds sat on the ribs of the carcass of a lion, and her mother sighed again. She picked a piece of confetti from the sauce and stared absently into the distance before finally licking it from her finger. 'There's something ominous on the way. She's keeping something from me, I know my daughter,' she repeated as she left and swallowed hard. 'She can't look me in the eyes . . .'

*

Luisa put the book back on the shelf, slipped into her ballet shoes and straightened her skirt. Then she strolled around the big rooms, lit by shaded lamps and candelabras. Most of the wallpaper was floral, and many of the women on the armchairs and sofas had spread their flouncy frocks so wide that they lay on the knees of their uniformed companions. While the men talked to one another or sipped their drinks, they kept glancing furtively at her, which made her uneasy and once caused her to trip over the edge of a mat. But then she heard her father's voice and exhaled. 'Never!' he exclaimed behind the swinging kitchen door. 'It was aquavit! Ice-cold water of life!'

A tiled, slightly gloomy room. In the background, by the stoves, lamps shone through the cooks' caps. Grilled chickens turned on several spits, and dripping fat burned with a bluish flame. Her father's forehead was glistening, his tie hung at an angle, and the two men he was sitting with at a table were clearly no longer sober; their cheeks were red, their eyes glazed, and he smiled at his daughter, put an arm around her waist and said, 'Gentlemen, in case the unexpected brightness dazzles you: Luisa Norff, the light of my loins.'

An officer in a dark-blue uniform, with the Iron Cross on his chest, tapped the brim of his cap; he was about thirty, with the hint of a reddish beard. The other man, who wore his tie tied short and had sleeve rubbers on his shirt, had just lit a cigarette and was putting the charred match back in the Jupiter pack, and her father said: 'And these, my love, are my new friends: Herr Klettenberg, Oberleutnant zur See, and Dr Sievert from . . . What's the name of your office again?'

The other man, slightly younger than Luisa's father, in his early fifties but already greying, waved his hand. His neck and the back of his hands were scattered with slightly raised patches like a nettle rash. 'The Reich Armaments Office,' he said and puffed out smoke sharply from the corner of his mouth. 'Materials testing. Boring stuff.'

Holding the cognac bottle, he studied the label, and the officer laughed, a sardonic sound. He pushed his cap off his forehead, and unlike the stubble of his beard his hair was light blond. 'Materials testing? That's a joke. That's pencil sharpeners! None of those people have ever held a piece of steel in their hands, let alone a gun. But they all know how to shoot their load! Without Vaseline.' He looked at Luisa with apparent regret. 'If you'll forgive my French!'

Even though she hadn't understood the meaning of the officer's words, she couldn't help smiling; she thought he was nice. But the official ignored the lieutenant, raised his brandy glass and said to her father: 'It certainly wasn't aquavit, believe me. Remembering things is my job. We were all given water, as always when the Grand Admiral is there. He only drinks Fachinger mineral water, in fact. Liver problems, hepatitis B.'

Luisa's father took a stool out from under the sink and she sat down between him and the officer, who drained his glass in one draught. 'Clever fellow, that Dönitz, you'd have to admit. An icy gaze. The men have always looked up to him, even when he was just a commodore,' he murmured. 'He never made them do anything he wouldn't have done himself. And no extras; when the caboose was empty, it was rusks for him too! So you can even forgive him that vain radio announcement about his new rank . . . But now he just has to use us up, boat after boat. What else is he supposed to do?'

Sievert thoughtfully studied his fingers, the hives on them. 'Come on now . . . This is defeatism, isn't it? Our new torpedoes will sort everything out. They're almost a miracle weapon, Dönitz said.'

The officer grunted. 'Nonsense, man! They might look that way from your desks. But you can forget about that sonar location that costs God knows how many million! As if the English were stupid. They'll take a long washing-line, hang a few rattles on the line that are louder than the engine and those things of yours will whir away into the void! It's called an effective enemy repellent, and it costs practically nothing!' With his elbow on the sink, he looked over at the grill and called, 'When will those flutterers be done? When I'm pissed I don't need a reason, damn it!'

One of the cooks said something but Luisa wasn't listening. She tugged at her father's sleeve and said quietly: 'Dad, I don't feel well. I've got a terrible headache . . .

149

Didn't you want to go home early?' She pointed at the half-empty bottle. 'If you drink any more you won't be able to drive us.'

Her father ran a reassuring hand over her hair and was about to say something, but Klettenberg struck the table. 'Home? Who wants to go home? In wartime nobody's tired, obviously!' He pointed at the official with his thumb. 'Apart from these pen-pushers here. They're always asleep. What was that about the Grand Mineral? What sort of water doesn't he like?'

Sievert looked around; there was red scurf around his ears as well. 'Now I need my jacket . . . I've got a photograph in it, Lübeck mariners' guild '41. Our whole department and Dönitz eating cabbage. Terrific speech. And there wasn't a single glass of alcohol on the table, not one!'

'Well,' said Luisa's father, 'since then senior officers have had ample reason to drink something other than Seltzer water, don't you think? At any rate, in my local he recently ordered various coffees topped up with plenty of rum!' He grinned. 'Strictly speaking that counts as an official secret, gentlemen, but he was even listing a little. But he always had a first-rate posture on deck, I'd have to say.'

Fat hissed in the pan, and Klettenberg drained his glass and wiped his mouth with the back of his hand. 'Of course he got drunk! It would be sad if he didn't. He's still a human being, damn it all, not an object of materials analysis. He has weaknesses and makes mistakes.'

Sievert scratched both of his wrists at the same time. 'Oh, really? And what might those have been?' he asked mockingly, with his cigarette in his mouth. 'Because he overlooked you for promotion, or what?'

Two gold stripes and a star flashed on the officer's sleeve. 'Nonsense,' he replied. 'Just normal mistakes, the kind the Führer would make if he had the wrong advisers.' He smacked the other man's white cap onto his head. 'People like you, for example: stupid specialists who don't even know what a wind direction is, and who piss all over their own feet.'

Then he raised his glass, and the official took a big soup ladle from the basket beside the table. 'Well, now I'm excited,' he said, studied himself in the reflecting bulge and adjusted his hair. 'What exactly do you mean?'

'Oh, God, what could he mean,' Luisa's father sighed. 'That we're all imperfect, or what? Can I top you up, gentlemen?'

Only Klettenberg held out his glass; as he did so he looked at the official. 'I can tell you exactly what I mean, you clot. I come from Wilhelmshaven, I've never seen anything but ships as long as I've lived. And as a child there was only one thing I wanted to be: a naval officer. I've always liked the polish, the clarity in those people's eyes and minds. They don't need culture, they have the sea, do you get that? A marine will never be a primitive butcher.'

Sievert stubbed out his cigarette. 'Well nobody says otherwise,' he said. 'And no one demands it either. Or what are you suggesting?'

He wiped his watch-glass with a moistened thumb, and the other man waved his hand. 'I'm not suggesting anything, but listen: I'm a sailor, I'm loyal and I would walk through fire for my commanding officer. But there are rules on the sea, written rules, they're there for all to read, and unwritten ones, they're the most important; they're the ones that tell you what kind of a fellow someone is. And one of those rules is: the crew of a sunken enemy ship are taken to safety if they're floating in the sea, they are supplied with food and drinking water if they are drifting around in lifeboats. That's been an iron rule for as long as there have been sea battles. And now guess what kind of order our honoured senior commander, the Grand Admiral by Hitler's graces, has issued as soon as he's up to his neck in shit . . . Well? If that isn't the purest nonsense! How do you think the enemy's dealing with us now?'

He knocked his cognac back again and bared his teeth with a groan. Then he leaned towards Luisa and murmured: 'You've got to stop stepping on my toes, kid. Or are you drunk too?'

She was deeply startled, whispered an apology and tilted her torso sideways to look under the table. Her father, whose shoes were much closer to the sailor's, grabbed her by the back of the neck, which might have looked like a loving gesture; but he pressed hard. As he did so he closed his eyes for a moment, a mute request for consideration, and said, 'She's got a headache and she's tired, Lieutenant, and that always makes her fidgety. She's been kicking away at my instep too . . .'

Something was being flambéed in the background, and the official on the other side of the table massaged his temples as he stared at the ceiling, where pots and pans hung on meat-hooks. 'Vain radio announcement, idiotic orders . . .

Those were your words, weren't they? But yes, what are they going to do at such times, times that are harsher than any pang of conscience. As experience teaches us, things that go down come back up again. Nothing is eaten so hot . . . I'm sure you know commanders who deliberately ignored his instructions and failed to carry them out, isn't that so?'

With his head tilted slightly to the side, he studied Klettenberg from the corner of his eye. Klettenberg swayed on his chair and raised his glass again, inflating his cheeks. He ran his fingertips over the tabletop, the jagged edge, and before he could say anything Luisa's father pushed back his chair and indicated that she should get up as well. 'As regards instructions, forgive me if I become less than convivial at this point, gentlemen: I request permission to leave. I have to go to Kiel tomorrow morning, and unload a night-ship.' He straightened his tie, extended a hand to Klettenberg and winked at the official. 'Danish aquavit.'

At that moment one of the cooks brought a big dish of crisply grilled chicken pieces to the table and set it down in front of the lieutenant, who groaned a silent 'Finally!' and fanned the aroma towards him with his cap. Then he unfolded a napkin and said to Sievert: 'It looks a picture, doesn't it? Immaculate! Even materials testing would have to sign off on that. Don't you want to help me? Come on, dig in!'

But the official, who said goodbye to the departing pair with a slack Hitler salute, shook his head. He ran his tongue over the bottom row of his teeth, then sniffed his cognac but didn't drink. 'No, no, just you eat,' he said, and his voice sounded as if his thoughts were elsewhere. 'You need your strength.'

*

In the drawing room Luisa's father picked up a beer from a tray. The waiter, the white-haired one in the tails that were too big for him, had once worked for her father, in a restaurant in Lübeck, and while the men talked to one another she ate a candied cherry she had taken from a shelf. 'Well, as we get older we all put on a few kilos,' her father said and wiped the foam from his mouth, 'what are you going to do?'

The waiter gave a melancholy sigh. 'But on the other hand our future declines,' he replied, and she stepped through the door into the smoking room and looked at her sister. She was the only one of the few women that evening who was wearing a tight dress, and one that only came down to her knee. With a cigarette in her right hand and a glass of wine in the other, she was chatting by the fire with some soldiers and civilians, and through the pale white fabric, with its fine embroidery, surrounding her hips and her narrow waist in a spiral, one could even make out the shape of her nipples.

On a marble table which was actually a chessboard a basket of oysters stood, and one of the men, an elderly soldier in a Wehrmacht uniform, was opening them with astonishing speed. He wedged them between the thumb and index finger of his left hand, a leather-covered prosthesis, and levered them open with his short combat knife.

Then he held out a plate to the people standing around him and said, 'Sylt royals. The last ones you'll see for a while.'

A bald SS officer with white piping on his black jacket drizzled lemon over the flesh, removed it with a fork and tried to feed it to Billie. He held it high over her open mouth and let the juice drip on her twitching tongue, but she kept turning away with a snort. The man in the dark flannel suit, the one who had met them at the buffet at the beginning, had put two of the greyish-yellow oysters behind the lenses of his glasses, and was making the slimy mass wobble with a gentle shake of his head. As he did so he pulled a fish face and made gurgling sounds, and Billie pressed her knees together and muttered, 'Stop it you idiot, I'm wetting myself!'

Her left stocking had a ladder on the calf, and the stray tendrils on the back of her head were now hanging down completely, exposing a finger-wide strip of velvet. The tall man with the white temples and the pearl on his tie wrapped his arm around her waist and tried to kiss her neck, and she screeched quietly and pushed him away. As she did so, something sloshed from her glass and dripped into her cleavage, and Luisa looked around for her father. But he was dancing with her mother, so she stepped into the room, tapped the inebriated girl on the back and hissed: 'You look dreadful. Adjust your hair!'

Her perfume had faded away almost completely, and Billie swayed slightly on her high heels and frowned uncomprehendingly. With a moist gleam in her eyes, she stubbed out the cigarette in an oyster shell and put her hand to the back of her head. Her lipstick was smudged too and, startled, she set down the white wine, picked up her bag from the mantelpiece and hurried into the corridor, where there was a guest bathroom. She seemed to feel the eyes of the men on her back; at any rate she made her hips swing a little too much. One of her strappy shoes was loose at the heel and she almost keeled over by the door, but caught herself on the handle.

The bespectacled man carefully released first one oyster and then the other from under his glasses, slurped them down and took a handkerchief out of his jacket. His lapel slipped to the side as he did so, and Luisa spotted a leather belt underneath it. 'Well, gentlemen,' he said under his breath, drying his cheeks and his fingers. His signet ring was decorated with two crossed anchors on a black background. 'The objective is agreed, the forces are collected. The moment couldn't be better. Who's going in first?'

He took out a flat case, and he didn't seem worried that Luisa had heard him, quite the contrary. With his eyes narrowed above the white scar on his face, he studied her from top to toe so coldly that it took her breath away and she fled backwards into the drawing room, nearly knocking over a vase on the floor. The man held out his cigarettes to the others, and she liberated a few thorny twigs with rosehips from her woollen jacket and stood on tiptoes, but couldn't see her parents among the dancers.

A woman withdrew her hand from the back of her cavalier's neck and pushed her gently away, and she slipped quickly beneath a waiter's tray and followed her sister into the corridor. Faint were the lamps burning on the walls, the door of the guest bathroom was locked, and Billie didn't reply to her knock and her quiet call. The sound of heels rang out on the tiles, a hectic back and forth, there was the sound of rushing water and something made of glass seemed to fall into the wash basin, perhaps her perfume bottle. Because after a moment of silence the scent of fresh perfume came through the cracks: gardenia.

*

Rhythmic clapping could be heard in the drawing room. The musicians were playing a popular-song version of the 'Badenweiler' march, and as she waited Luisa studied the framed engravings on the wall, medieval battle scenes. Mercenaries with plumed hats rode their horses over corpses that covered the field all the way to the horizon. Smoke poured from all the houses and barns, a dozen men hung from a tree, children too, and two soldiers of fortune were pouring fluid into a funnel inserted into a woman's mouth.

Her broken teeth lay beside her head, her girlish body was full of slit-like wounds, and Luisa gave a start when she felt a hand on the back of her neck and a breath in her ear. 'That's my birthday present!' Vinzent said as he drew her to him again. 'And you're creeping around all by your-self in the dusk . . . Are you bored?'

The shiny silk lapel of his jacket was cool to her cheek, and even though he looked clean-shaven his chin scratched on her forehead. 'No, why?' Luisa answered. 'I'm never bored.'

He laughed. 'Oh, really? That's good. That's even enviable. Always curious, yes? Always open to . . .'

He pointed at the spiral staircase at the end of the corridor. A sign hung over the banister with a downward-pointing arrow and the letters LSR on the wall, and he sniffed her hair and said, 'Didn't you want to see the new bunker? You'll be amazed, I can promise you that. All excellent quality, with a radio, bar and bunk bed, and of course it's gas-proof. They could drop a whole bomber on our roof and you would still sleep like a baby down there.'

But Luisa wriggled from his clutches. 'Thank you, maybe some other time. I'm just waiting for the bathroom to be free. Billie's quite drunk . . . And we're leaving soon.'

By the light of the little parchment-shaded lamps above the engravings his eyes looked weary, dulled with alcohol; the vertical folds between his eyebrows also gave his expression a menacing quality. 'You're doing what? Why? I'm just starting to find you ravishing. What didn't you like? Was the food bad? The musicians are a bit boring, aren't they? You can only get invalids these days. But later, once the security service men have gone, I'm sure they'll play some swing!'

He swayed his hips and snapped his fingers, and Luisa said, 'No! Dad thought it was lovely too, honestly. I don't feel very well, I've been having headaches all day and I'm worn out, I have no idea why. And he has to go to Kiel early tomorrow morning.'

Again Vinzent put an arm around her shoulders and darted a look into the drawing room. 'Of course . . . But I'm not a monster, I don't want you to suffer at my party,' he replied and pushed her towards the stairs. She could feel his cufflink through her woollen jacket. 'There's a well-equipped pharmacy with all kinds of pills in the bunker. We'll find something for you. Mind the steps.'

Luisa was at a loss, and swallowed hard. To put up more than inward resistance struck her as impolite. He was the host, and her brother-in-law at that, and the idea that her reserve might insult him worried her more than the basement; still she said, halfway down the stairs: 'Wait! Billie must be nearly ready. Then we could take her too, couldn't we?'

He nodded and strengthened his grip, apparently concerned to keep her from falling. 'She knows it already,' he said, and in the stairwell his voice sounded darker than it was. 'She's always found it cosy down here.'

Behind the steel door with the inscription 'Air Raid Shelter Smoking Forbidden!' a faintly lit, whitewashed corridor began. It was long, with axes and shovels on the walls and bright red arrows painted on the stone floor, but not very wide, and it narrowed even further in the places where sandbags for extinguishing phosphorus bombs lay stacked in waist-high piles. The surface of the water in the buckets was dark with dust and twitched rhythmically.

The stamping and clapping in the rooms grew quieter and, alarmed, Luisa gasped for air: her knees gave way and the arrows seemed to slip away beneath her as soon as the heavy door had fallen shut. Vinzent had vigorously lifted her onto the sandbags, uttering a strange sound, a playful growl. His shadow loomed over her, his bow tie brushed her cheek and in her horror she didn't know whether to laugh or scream. 'No, stop that!' she hissed. 'We'll get all dirty.'

She struck at him with both hands, weak with disbelief. But he only grinned, and she turned her face away under his stubbly cheeks and was pursing her lips when something wet passed against them, something spittle-warm that reminded her of the foul-smelling corners of her mother's handkerchief. At the same time she felt his fingers between her thighs, his fingernails in the skin above her woollen stockings, she let out a bit of urine out of fear and panted, 'Stop, now! Go away!' She pulled his head back by the hair. 'I'll tell your wife!'

Then he lay on her entirely with his broad chest, muttered something through his teeth that she couldn't make out and gripped her throat; she couldn't even swallow now, and lowered her hands. Breathless and as frozen as that time when she fell from the swing in Kiel, she could feel the lower part of his body, something hard in his pocket, opened her mouth and looked up at the swaying light bulb. The tungsten filament appeared multiplied through her tears, a glowing smear.

She closed her eyes tight and inhaled Vinzent's hot breath. The man's probing tongue, which tasted of schnapps and tobacco, made her ill, and so did his hot spittle as it trickled into her mouth, and she couldn't help burping slightly, gastric acid rising into her nose. Then she belched and felt a moment later as if she was going to bring up her lemon tart; she struggled and kicked. And finally her brother-in-law gave in, raised his chin and peered at her through narrowed eyes. He looked quite angry.

With her head turned towards the wall, she let the fluid run from the corners of her mouth. Her pulse thumped in her throat and her breathing was so violent that it stirred the flaking scraps of paint on the wall. Vinzent got to his feet, knocked the dust from his trousers and tugged on his sleeves. He was almost level with the light bulb, and even though the sandbags were damp she went on lying there and looked up at him from the corner of her eye. It was hard to swallow, and something hurt in her throat. 'Was that a French kiss?' she asked hoarsely. 'Are you going to rape me?'

He laughed seriously through his nose and handed her a carefully folded handkerchief, a white square. Her hand was trembling, and she felt his embroidered initials on her lips when she wiped her mouth. 'Yes, that was a kiss,' he said. 'That's how grown-ups do it, you'll come to like it. And nobody's being raped here, where do you get such ideas? Are they in your novels?'

He craned his neck, straightened his bow tie and ran his hands through his tousled hair. Then he came so close to the sacks that she smelled the ironing water of his dinner jacket, a hint of lavender. She could see into his bristly nostrils, and when he looked down at her his eyes were strangely vacant. 'We're not barbarians, we're relatives, isn't that right? We're doing this as a family arrangement, child. I do something for you, you do something for me. You know what I mean?'

He grinned again. The sound that his manicured nails

produced on the horn buttons of his trousers was like the breaking of tiny bones, and suddenly she felt as if she were lying on a pile of cold animals. She quickly sat up, pushed something aside on the sandbags and stared at his hand, rummaging behind the black fabric. Only his little finger with the silver death's-head ring worn by SS officers peered from the slit.

Above them a moth flew against the light, the clear glass rang out quietly under its whirring wings, dust rustled down and, shivering, she folded her arms in front of her chest and said as calmly as she could: 'Did you really shoot the pilot that time?'

Vinzent gave a barely perceptible start and closed and opened his eyelids several times. Droplets of sweat glistened on his forehead and upper lip, and when he lowered his head slightly, the dark blue of his eyes looked black. 'I did what? Who do you mean?'

One of her hairs stood out on his shoulder. 'Well, the young Englishman who had the forced landing in the Halifax in front of the convent. He was injured, he had blood coming from his head and you chatted. And then you disappeared with him behind the hull, and I heard a bang that sounded like a pistol shot. Did you really kill him and throw him into the Alte Eider?'

He didn't reply, or only with a frown. 'Dad said that's against the Geneva Convention,' she went on hastily. 'Just like the murder of the pilots in Borkum. The Allies will bring every single perpetrator up before the military court. On the Rhine, where the Americans are, and among the English and the Canadians in Holland that's already happening. Even doctors and orderlies who didn't treat crashed pilots and let them die will be going to the gallows, he said.'

The moth fell on the floor with a papery sound and lay there awkwardly, and now Vinzent sighed, pulled his hand from his trousers and slowly buttoned up his fly. 'Is that so? Well, this is news!' he murmured and smelled his fingers, looking thoughtfully at the girl. 'It's almost frightening, isn't it?'

Even though there was a sign saying 'No smoking' at the end of the corridor, he drew a Juno from the pack and searched for his lighter. 'So listen,' he said. 'First of all he wasn't a pilot, he was just a radio operator. And even though fellows like that, those terrorist airmen, are destroyers of our cities and murderers of innocent women and children: I would certainly not be so undignified as to hand them to the lynch mob. What do you think people would have done with him? They've all heard Goebbels' speeches, you could have scraped him off the road!' He pressed his thumb on his gold Zippo. 'And thanks to my compassion he was spared that.'

Luisa closed her fist around the handkerchief. Again her eyes grew moist. 'So it's true?' she asked quietly. 'You did it.'

He shook his head and sighed irritably. 'Oh, my little milkmaid, what can I tell you. We're at war, you have orders to obey even if you don't like them. You're best off shooting at their backs, between their shoulder blades; it goes so quickly – he doesn't even know he's dead. Then in the daily report it says "shot while escaping", and we can all live with that. We have avenged our people, and don't need to feed him as a prisoner. And should the wind of history turn, his people can believe that he actually died while fleeing, a hero. Come over here . . .'

He sat down beside her on the sacks, took his handkerchief and carefully dried her eyes. 'People don't want to know things like that, do they? You stay in your world of books, stories and poems and you can stay away from it all. They have nothing to do with real life . . .' He drew on the cigarette and inhaled deeply. '. . . but there has to be room for simplicity too.'

Luisa, who had forgotten long since that she was wearing make-up, looked at the high-class fabric with the mascara stains in her hand. What she had originally taken for embroidered initials was a tiny swastika, white on white, and suddenly the light went out, and the music beyond the steel door fell silent too; there was the sound of shocked exclamations and drunken screeches. But Vinzent didn't react, and went on sitting calmly where he was. 'It'll be light soon,' he murmured.

She felt his hand on her knee, the soft plucking at her stocking. 'So now we too have a secret, who would have thought it. It could be a lovely spring. Incidentally, I guessed a long time ago that something in you had awoken, not just physically; men sense that. Your curious glances told me everything. But thank God you're not like your sister, you don't just throw yourself away, do you? And you know very well when it's better to keep your mouth shut.'

She wanted to edge away from him, but didn't dare move. The glow lit up his hollow hand when he drew on his cigarette again. 'And while we're on the subject of gossip. That the Americans have already reached the Rhine and the Canadians are in Holland, organizing trials of pilots and even lynching doctors and orderlies – that is sadly not untrue,' he went on. 'And that dreadful business on Borkum . . . My God, he was a poor lance corporal, whose whole family had been bombed to death, mother, daughter, pregnant wife. Who can blame him for being furious and emptying his magazine when he saw enemies whose planes had crashed? Isn't that only human?'

Somewhere in the basement rooms, presumably behind the bunker door, an engine was turned on, and there was a smell of petrol. The light came flickering on again, and Vinzent closed one eye, which made the gaze of the other more piercing. 'But there's one thing that interests me: there's an embargo, child, a news embargo, imposed from very high up. No one can know all of these things, certainly not your beloved father, who is anything but tight-lipped. So who hasn't been keeping mum? Hm?'

With his hand still on her thigh he increased his pressure, tilted his head to one side and looked at her expectantly. She swallowed, gnawed the inside of her lips, and stared at his upholstered shoulders, at the shiny lapel with the Party badge, the crystal buttons of his shirt. Its collar, she knew from her father, who wore a similar one, was called a shark collar, and in her imagination it was kept in shape by bones.

The music started up again, and dancing feet could be heard, the rhythmic stamping of a new conga, when at last she slipped from the sandbags and stood in front of her brother-in-law, between his knees. She wanted to cry, but there were no tears for the sadness that she felt, so she tried to smile. Vinzent threw his cigarette butt into the fire bucket, she plucked her hair from his dinner jacket and then closed her eyelids and stopped resisting his strength, the stubble that made her skin sting, the hand that guided hers.

It happened very quickly, he gritted his teeth and sank against the wall, and while she dried her fingers with his handkerchief and tried to ignore the smell, she noticed the delicate imprint of her eyelashes on the cambric. Like the torn-off legs of flies.

*

She kept the bathroom door locked for a long time, washed her hands over and over again and rinsed out her mouth. In the brush by the mirror, which was full of grey hairs, there were also a few red ones, but she straightened her hair with her spread fingers. Then she walked again through the rooms, looking out for her parents. There were already gaps between the officers' caps on the shelves and windowsills, with empty glasses standing in them. There was no staff behind the buffet, almost all the bowls and pans were empty, the wild boar bone scraped clean. The old waiter was smoking by the canal.

She found her father in the billiards room, by a black card table; he immediately threw down his hand and stood up when he saw her. Three elegantly dressed women and an old man, their faces waxy with concentration, raised their heads for a moment but said nothing, and he led his daughter into the drawing room and murmured: 'There's nothing more pathetic than card players who are concerned with winning. After a certain age you should know that there's nothing, really nothing, to lose. You look bad, child, somehow preoccupied. Where have you been?'

A record was playing, and Luisa made a vague gesture and linked arms with him as they walked around the dancers to the little bar in the bay window. Nets, pennants and a stuffed swordfish with coins in its eye sockets hung from the ceiling, and her mother, a liqueur glass in her hand, was chatting with two musicians. They were both wearing uniforms that were plainly new, a freshly ironed field grey with green velvet cuffs.

'Oh, there he is,' she said. 'I was just telling these gentlemen about our house.' She drained her glass and set it down on the counter next to an abandoned trumpet. 'So it's a terraced house, but very smart and spacious, and I say to this one here: yes, it might well have been a dead hit, but not everything will have gone up in flames. There must be a few souvenirs, personal things, go and look. Which he did. But what does he bring me? Family jewels? Our love letters? A photograph of the children? No, a vase, can you imagine? A horribly ugly brown flower vase as the last memory of our happy life!'

'Very touching,' her husband interrupted. 'That's probably exactly what these gentlemen are interested in. Here, look after your little one, she's got a headache. I'll go and find the other one, and then we can set off.'

'Touching indeed,' his wife said through her teeth, pulled her stole together in front of her chest and stamped her heel on the floor. 'Pitiful and pathetic it was! The vase didn't even belong to us!'

Her husband waved her words away and she watched furiously after him. But then the laughter of the musicians seemed to placate her; smiling, she touched Luisa's forehead. 'What is it, mademoiselle, why so pale? And with a slight temperature, I would say. Probably the champers. Or perhaps you've been reading too much in your hidey-hole again and need glasses?'

The sailor behind the bar put on a new record, something by Ise Werner, and she laid an arm around her waist and swayed back and forth for a moment. 'Thank you, my eyesight's fine,' Luisa said, pulling her torso away. 'And I haven't drunk any sparkling wine either. Oh and by the way you can let go of me. I don't want you to do that!'

Humming along with the tune, Luisa's mother took the girl's left hand and drew her into a spin. 'What is it you want? And why not?'

The parquet creaked under them. 'Because I don't want it! I think it's awful when women dance together. It looks so sad.'

Her mother nodded. 'Well, if you mean those poor widows in Café Overbeck, you might even be right. What else are they supposed to do? And how is that going to look after the war? But a mother can dance with her daughter; it's part of her education. Come on, shift your chassis. Isn't that nice?'

'No,' Luisa said, 'stop it! I'll only step on your toes. Let's go home, please. I really have a headache, and I feel ill too.'

'Oh, my God, that endless whining noise! Have I brought nothing but divas into the world? We're going in a minute. You have no idea how everything aches. And round to the left, and a dos-a-dos, and . . . Why should you be having headaches anyway?'

Luisa shrugged and looked furtively around. She was brushed several times by skirts and uniform jackets, and one couple or another came menacingly close to her with their elbows sharply bent. But that didn't seem to bother her mother; eyes closed, she guided her through the tune and sang the refrain, her voice a little deeper and hoarser than Werner's: 'It is my heart's premiere, the play is called: You and Me, and resist though I might, my heart beats for you alone!'

The naval lieutenant with the blond hair and the reddish stubble came out of the kitchen. He was plainly so drunk that he could no longer walk on his own; two officers in coats, both wearing serious expressions, helped him through the drawing room. He tripped over a chair leg, a wooden paw, his cap slipped onto his ear, and when he tried to raise a hand to straighten it, the handcuffs were revealed, the fetter on his wrist. But none of the dancers seemed to pay any attention; they looked into each other's eyes and turned smiling away from the tableau, back into the popular tune.

Her mother did the same. Hanging in the old chandelier, whose crystal droplets were either opaque or dark brown like rock candy, were a few paper streamers, and they danced past the door to the smoking room. The carpet was scattered with oyster shells and lemon halves, and the man with the white temples and the pearl in his tie winked at her from his deep leather armchair. He even raised his glass, and only now did Luisa notice the stain on the arm of her woollen jacket, glistening like a snail trail. She gasped, a quivering inhalation, and said close to her mother's ear: 'You know Vinzent's a swine, don't you?'

Her mother abruptly broke off her humming and wrinkled her painted eyebrows. 'What? What's up with you? Move a little more fluidly, child, have you swallowed a broom? Once the war's over, the first thing you're going to have is dancing classes!'

Then she smiled dreamily and nodded towards the hand-painted wallpaper, the red and purple flowers, divided by brass strips. 'Do you remember the lupins in our garden? The ones behind the swing? When you were five you used to call them lupians, with an extra a, because you thought it sounded nicer. And Pastor Schimmel was known as Bimmel.'

Luisa shook her head. 'I say lupians even today,' she said. 'Please stick to the subject.'

Her mother, with a mildly serious expression on her face, looked at her in silence for three steps. Then she took a deep breath. 'Yes, are you off on a morality jag now, or what's going on?' she said quietly. 'Be careful not to rush to judgement. Vinzent is a man of honour, he has style and manners. And if you mean that thing with Billie: your sister is an adult and can do what she likes, she always has done. These days lots of people do all kinds of things for extra rations or a pretty dress. Why do you think we're kept so well supplied and don't have to go and work in the cattle sheds? And why haven't any refugees been put in our flat? Well? Think about that!'

The song was over, and she stood there like everyone else, waiting for the record to change, but kept hold of Luisa and muttered: 'He may be a daredevil, my handsome son-in-law, who even I could fall for. But he's certainly not a swine, child. He always speaks extremely highly of you, and you owe it to him that you're doing your land-girl year here and not in some Polish pub in West Prussia where the Russians would have raped you long ago.' Smiling, she closed her pale blue eyelids. 'So to some extent does Sibylle too . . .'

Violins and quiet choral singing started up, voices coming as if over water, and she brushed a tendril of hair over her youngest daughter's ear. 'Oh, Lulu, let's be honest: our eldest may be a model national comrade and a whatsit-Führerin, but she's certainly not the warmest of souls,' she went on. 'She completely used up her first fiancé, that young teacher. So it can hardly come as a surprise if her husband, at the height of his powers, should seek other hunting grounds . . . Well now. And since she's been pregnant, she's become more and more cold and calculating. You can see it: she constantly avoids me, she hasn't exchanged a word with me all evening, she hasn't introduced me to a soul. She's ashamed of us, of the whole family. I have to make do with the staff.'

Behind the counter the sailor turned up the volume and then Hans Albers sang 'La Paloma', and she gripped Luisa tighter again and said, 'Come on, off we go. Get some air under those feet of yours! Lift your knees! By the way you can't make mistakes when you're dancing, the only thing you mustn't be is shy. Step on your cavalier's toes, throw him off beat with a head-butt by all means, but always smile in his face. Let your sister show you.' She raised her chin and looked around. 'Where's she got to? Wasn't your father going to collect her?'

The stole slipped from her neck, where her powder had formed tiny crumbs, and Luisa clung tightly to her. Beyond the silhouettes of the broad-shouldered men and their flounce-skirted wives the violin music, now accompanied by an accordion, sounded like a twilight to her. Precisely because he clearly couldn't sing and could hardly hold a note, Hans Albers' rough voice touched her deeply, and on the lines 'Longing pulls me away to the blue distance / sea below me, above me night and stars' tears even came to her eyes. But luckily the record was scratched.

*

Her father waved at them and tapped his watch, and with relief Luisa pulled her mother from the dance floor. Other people were leaving too, in the frame of the painting in the foyer, the huge wheat field, there were dozens of visiting cards, and her father shrugged his shoulders, turned down the corners of his mouth and said: 'No idea where our prima donna can have got to. Come on, let's go while the weather is bearable.'

Each time the front door opened and let in a gust of wind, an air-raid siren could be heard in the distance, and Gudrun, who had clearly freshened herself up – her lipstick was pale, her Olympic roll glossy – came quickly down the stairs. 'What's this, are we off already?' she asked, apparently perplexed, and spread her arms out. 'But that's a shame, isn't it? We can hardly talk amongst all this commotion! Were you not feeling well? Karl's still on his way, the Grand Admiral; the Ochsenweg was blocked. I'm sure he'll give a speech.'

After helping her mother into her coat, Luisa's father slipped into his own, swaying slightly. 'I'm afraid I know it already,' he murmured and cleared his throat. 'We've been feeling absolutely marvellous, my dear, many thanks!' he continued in a louder voice. 'Stimulating people, delicious food, lovely music. But just look at how poorly the little one is, how perfectly gastric she looks. And I have to go to Kiel very early tomorrow morning . . . Where, then, is our host, so that we may take our leave in an orderly fashion?'

Luisa's mother put her hat on and peered into the adjacent room. The gold pheasant feather was bent and dangled over one of her ears, although she didn't notice. 'Just a moment, we're not going without Billie,' she said. 'Have you really looked everywhere?'

He looked up at the ceiling. 'No,' he replied, 'of course I wasn't allowed to go into the bedrooms, they were occupied. Soldiers on leave from the front make use of every bedspring to refresh the army. Now, please, come on. Usually you're the one who lets her do whatever she likes. Let her enjoy her own party; a suitor is bound to bring her home. Probably several.'

Luisa had waited in the foyer many times before; but this evening she saw the sanded spot on the massive newel post for the first time. Even though it had been stained dark brown to match the whole staircase and the panelling, the star of David was still just visible. Her mother stared broodingly into the distance for a moment, moving her lips mutely. 'No, no, that's impossible, that's entirely out of the question. Under no circumstances are we leaving Billie behind,' she repeated and gave Luisa a sign. 'You go and look. And give her a piece of your mind if she doesn't come with us.'

At this the young cloakroom attendant turned towards them. She was the one with the crown braid, and she hung a few empty hangers on the rack and said, 'I'm sorry, are you talking about the red-haired lady in the white taffeta gown, about my height? I gave her scarf and coat half an hour ago. Astrakhan collar, yes? She drove off with Herr Streeler.'

Gudrun nodded. 'With Captain Streeler,' she corrected her with a smile and showed the pink palms of her hands. 'And with that the mystery is solved. The dashing Rainald has hit today's jackpot! At least she has taste, he always smells so pleasantly of birch water. He might be married and a bit short-sighted, but his duelling scar makes a good impression. And as a cavalier he knows what is expected of him, and he will bring her home safe and sound. With an amorous delay, I assume.'

She opened the door and said, only apparently for Luisa's benefit: 'That's how it is with flighty girls, isn't it? First much ado about nothing, then gone with the wind.'

The candles on the outside steps had gone out; another air-raid siren could now be heard in Rendsburg. Wrinkling his nose, her father looked into the sky. 'I knew it, horrible weather on the way,' he said and took his stepdaughter by the hand. 'So, to be honest, I'd rather have a flighty girl in the family, dearest, than an earthbound boy. And incidentally, do you know what my oh-so-rejected daughter has over you? Do you want to know?'

He pinned his Party badge back on the inside of his lapel and buttoned up his coat, and Gudrun, seemingly holding both hands protectively in front of her belly, raised her chin. Her lips were narrow, her gaze unmoving, and the pale skin of her face tensed as if it were about to turn to marble. 'She is absolutely honest,' he went on. 'She says what she thinks, lives what she feels and takes what she needs – even if it's another girl's boyfriend. Kindest regards!'

Then his wife hit him on the back of his neck with her gloves. 'There you go again, you dunderhead. Always those blue jokes of yours!' she exclaimed and gave a childish wave, a quick bend of the fingers. 'See you soon, then, darling, it was wonderful. I'm so happy that we're allowed to be here. Many, many thanks! And come and see us soon. Now that you're making me a grandmother I absolutely need to know how you are. Oh heavens, all this anticipation! I hope you will be spared varicose veins. They run in the family . . .'

A ship's foghorn somewhere on the canal, echoing in the empty silos. The gravel on the forecourt crunched under their shoes. The light from the hallway cast a dull light on the low boxwood balls, which appeared at one spot to have been stepped on or driven over, and while her parents climbed into the car and the engine started, Luisa glanced back at the door. Gudrun was already saying goodbye to other guests, and she bent down quickly and detached the pincushion from the bent branches. It smelled of gardenia.

*

The pains hadn't eased, on the contrary. Her head felt as if it was on fire, her pulse throbbed in her ears. But she could hear the whinnying and the hammering hooves in the distance when she came out of the dairy the next day. Cold rain was falling, rattling loudly on the roof of the big brown furniture van that stood by the pasture in the park. 'Wool collection', it said on the side, 'Don't save – sacrifice!' and, whistling and clapping, several soldiers in rubber boots drove the horses up the ramp. Some slipped on the muddy planks and tried to turn around, but the men struck the thin legs with clubs, and with their rifle butts too, making the bones ring out as though they were hollow.

They shooed the whinnying animals into the narrowing space with the oval skylight where, pressed closely together, they stretched their necks so that they could breathe. Among them was Breeze, her whole body quivering, her legs covered with dung, and Luisa knocked on the door of the removal van and asked the driver where the horses were being taken to. A white-haired civilian, with a stub of cardboard between his lips, he looked up from his newspaper, the *Eider Kurier*, but said nothing. He ran his thumb along his throat and went on turning the pages, and she stared in disbelief at the hoof-prints in the mud, which were already filling with water. Then she left the jug behind and ran across the yard.

She rang and knocked at the administrator's door at the same time; Frau Thamling opened it and gave her a questioning look. Her heart was racing so much that she couldn't say a word, she pointed breathlessly towards the pasture, and the frail woman pulled her inside by the sleeve. 'Nice and calm,' she said. 'Take a deep breath, little one. What do you mean, the horses? Terrible, I know, but there's nothing we can do about it, nothing at all. The army supply office . . . Meat for the front. If we could only keep one of them here . . .' Puzzled, she leaned forward. 'What's wrong with your eyes? Come into the light.'

She turned a switch and asked Luisa to stick her tongue out. It was strawberry-coloured at the edges and the tip, but had a whitish coating in the middle, as Luisa could see in the hall mirror, and Frau Thamling quickly unbuttoned her coat, her woollen jacket and the collar of her blouse and revealed what she herself hadn't yet noticed: from her neck to her breasts Luisa's skin was covered with tiny spots, from bright red to purple, which disappeared briefly when pressed and didn't itch. Still she immediately felt a desire to scratch them, and Frau Thamling held her hand tightly and said, 'Child, child, where did you catch this!'

As if the mirror in the warm flat had been struck by a breath of ice, Luisa suddenly saw everything as if through a fog. Her legs grew weak, a rotten taste filled her mouth and she slumped on a chair. The noise in her intestines embarrassed her; with her arms folded over her belly she murmured an apology, but the woman seemed not to have heard a thing. She called for her husband, who came out of the room with the sky-blue painted ceiling and pulled a napkin from his shirt collar. She whispered something to him.

He too felt her forehead. His callused hand was cold, his light grey eyes wide with amazement, and his voice seemed to echo inside her as he said: 'Don't worry! It'll sort itself out!' Then he put one arm under her armpits and one under her knees, lifted her from the chair and carried her up the creaking stairs. 'It's bound to sort itself out!'

Winter passed agreeably amidst smoke and smouldering. The time when a stone was kinder to us than the heart of a soldier of fortune seemed to have passed for now. The afterglow of the comet of which everyone had spoken released the region from the tribulation of the armies, and the exiles carried their sparse belongings into the village on their bloody backs. Everything torn and ripped was mended, and the trunks filled up with grain and clothing aplenty. The warm spring did us good, the wood stayed dry and was easy to carve, which was necessary for the still nameless undertaking, and also for the consecration.

To the writer's puzzlement it was Johann, old Bubenleb, who gave the correct advice when he proclaimed: the saints, swathed in incense and gold leaf, have had enough of houses with elaborate altars! But oh, all skill for nothing! Because the three scourges, hunger, war and pestilence, rain down tirelessly upon us. The prayers that we send to heaven trickle back as ashes into our eyes, and now that is enough of the pious litanies, the sweet song, now we need a church for cursing! I want to build a tabernacle to pain, pallor and hesitancy, to the last vision of ravaged innocence.

For that reason we call this house 'The chapel of the ill-used maiden'!

Many are they who must have secretly crossed themselves when the wind made the reeds and branches crackle like the fires of the Inquisition: no one in the village dared to protest. Everyone thought of the young nun, of her blood on the altar, and the author of these lines could not fault his speech, since in its heart it was directed towards the Lord, towards holy mercy.

He felled the timber for his vessel, a flat-bottomed boat, he scorched the bow and tarred the hemp. The chapel was braced in all directions with birchwood to keep it from warping, and planked from without with rough beams. Then the master freed the oak corner pillars, so broad that they could be cut with the bow-saw, and laid round logs all the way to the shore, a long distance. And at last he summoned the people, a tattered, ragged mob who helped him willingly with his task, particularly when he promised them a party.

The telling of this is swifter than the building of it. Everyone was rewarded for their time with callused hands, and the hunger of the workers told of the strength that they needed. The wife of the cooper, old Milger, cooked up heaven knows what in huge pots; everything turned to pulp, good will included, and in the end no one knew whether they were eating frog-heads or fish-heads, everyone spat out the white eyes. She baked tooth-breakers and called them bread.

But then, miracle of miracles, the work was finished, the building slowly inclined, and anyone who came innocently from the forests with herbs or meagre kills on their belts and blinked into the morning sun: they could not believe their eyes when they saw a creaking little church, held by countless arms and ropes, sliding at an angle down the slope on wooden rollers to the shore. And the bell hung yet more crooked from the tower; but its sound was plumb.

Bringing the Lord's house to water was far from easy, because it weighed more than the carpenter had calculated. Once brought successfully to the boat, the vessel sank immediately to its immersion depth and no prayer could raise it; a sudden wind, a powerful wave, and the depths would have taken everything. But here too the master used his wisdom and quickly removed the door from its hinges, the heavy slates were taken from the roof-spars and the bell from the yoke. All of that could be carried over land, on springy planks through boggy marshes.

Then some boys, holding the ends of their ropes between their teeth, swam straight across the lake to the eastern shore, where two Haflinger horses snorted in their harnesses, draught-horses that had once hauled cannon, and would pull death no more. Even though they could hear again the armies beyond the forest, the battle-cries and the thunder of the cannons royal: now they drew sacred life. Quiet and constant the little towed church slid towards the village, to the hearts of those waiting for it to arrive, the water barely wrinkled before the bow, and where the writer of these lines beheld the light of the vision, dear Lord, how the tears did flow!

Dizziness and fog, her breathing quick and short. Her mouth was always dry, drink though she might, and the skin on her lips cracked; even contact with the edge of a glass was painful. Turning over in bed was often impossible, in her flickering dreams people lay on top of her, countless bodies in an overcrowded hospital. Then she hunched again in the burning heat as if between fireclay walls, which she was under no circumstances to touch, and gasped for air. And early in the morning she was woken by her own trembling, the chattering of her teeth, and her nightgown was so wet with sweat that it had to be rolled off her. The stripes of the mattress appeared through the sheet.

It was either her mother or Frau Thamling who washed her then and changed her bed. They wore grey overalls and rubber gloves and, too exhausted to open her eyes, she could mostly tell by the sounds and the smell who was working in the room at any time. Frau Thamling, quite silent, smelled of curd soap, cakes or fresh bread; her mother, clattering about with pans and bowls, of eau de cologne and cigarettes. Sometimes her father sat by her bed as well, held her fingers and talked to her, although she didn't understand much. But his voice was enough for her. He too wore rubber gloves.

The women tried to feed her, but she only occasionally ate some rusk, soaked in tepid milk, or a spoonful of yoghurt. There was a commode chair beside the bed, and what came out of her was almost odourless and looked like pea soup, run through with threads of blood. Her urine was also different from its usual colour, a deep dark amber, and as soon as she was finished she picked up the bell with the Christmas angel that had been put on her bedside table, and rang – or thought she rang. Often even a small turn of the hand was too much for her, and she fell wearily asleep.

'Dying for Beginners' she read on one of the paperbacks that Frau Mangoldt had left her, and one morning an old man with a hat, a beard and silver glasses came. He put a wooden stick in her mouth, examined her armpits, and gave her a few tiny white balls which she was to let dissolve on her tongue. They were sweet and got stuck between her teeth, and while she looked at the star, the patch on his coat jacket, with golden threads sticking out of it, he examined her hair between his fingers and said, 'Well, well, it's not so bad, *kinderlach*. Little Karl May survived it too!'

In spite of the bandage on her leg, which was replaced every half-hour, her fever mounted. She could seldom see clearly, and blinking or rubbing her eyes didn't help. Her pulse was so slow that she had a floating sensation between the beats, as if she were being gently lifted on a wave of warm air. Then again she had the feeling of falling deeply and even more deeply under the bed, into a bottomless space, and she clung tightly to the mattress. Every morning there was now a handful of hair on the pillow, and her mother wept and cursed the Jewish doctor. She combed it straight, tied it into strands and put them in a cigar box.

As long as Luisa heard heels on the wooden floor, the sound of a spoon in glass, metal sounds in general, the fiery heat became more bearable; it was only the silence that kept her from breathing. When, in spite of her blurred vision, she opened a book she seldom got beyond the first lines. Once Sister Mathilde came in and put a beautifully bound volume with a leather spine on the table: *The Chronicle of the Ochsenweg*. It was a dummy from the convent print-works, she explained, completely blank pages for sketches and notes, but Luisa had never heard the word before, and imagined it was a book for the time when she would no longer be able to speak, a volume for mute people, in fact, who invented stories of their own as they turned its pages. She put it under her pillow.

Once she dreamt that Gudrun had cut a dead calf from its mother, with a pair of secateurs. 'Do you think I'm going to let my marriage go to pot?' she said casually, with her arm in the animal up to the elbow, and Luisa exclaimed, 'But what sort of man sets his cap at all the girls?' The severed head appeared between the black labia, the long-lashed eyes, and her stepsister pulled it out of the cow by the ear and threw it in the straw. 'A rich man,' she replied. 'An influential one.'

The rows of little nodules on her throat and in her loins felt like subcutaneous strings of pearls, and sometimes, when the fever was particularly high, Luisa thought with pleasing clarity. Everything was formulated directly by her breath, and for the first time in her life she had a sense of her soul. It was an invisible colour, a quiet flowing on the spot, and she opened the dummy volume to record the thought. It already contained the phrase 'break spine', in her handwriting, which surprised her. Hadn't she written 'breath shrine'?

With her forehead pressed against the wall, the cool wallpaper, she heard Ole's voice; he wasn't allowed to enter the room. 'You can have my chestnut figures!' he shouted, and she nodded, so as not to insult him, and raised a grateful hand. He had brought fresh forsythia twigs from the garden. Frau Thamling put them on her bedside table, and as always in the spring, when Luisa saw such a twig or a bouquet, she plucked off a blossom and put it on her tongue – a little disappointed once again that something that was such a bright yellow didn't taste sweet. And now she thought that she might only have chosen the wrong one.

At one point she was woken by whinnying – or had it been a creaking door? Moonlight lay like snow on the furniture, and sometimes she sat up and looked in vain for her slippers. The heads of the nails in the cold floorboards were icier still, and she opened the wardrobe, put on her coat over her nightgown and left the room on tiptoes. Leaning against the banister, the scalloped handrail, she let herself slip down the stairs step by step. The fibres of the coconut runner pricked her soles, and she was panting when she pushed open the heavy front door and stepped outside between the columns of the porch.

For a moment she could make out the stars above the linden tree. There had been another frost, and she closed her eyes and opened her coat to let the wind refresh her. Chains rattled in the byre, and Motte, who was suddenly standing next to her, snuffled at her calves with his damp nose and wagged his tail. From a distance, presumably from the Baltic, came the sound of gunfire, and she slowly felt her way along the bright white facade, and only after a while did she understand that the slender shadow with the thin, transparent hair belonged to her.

The gate to the park was open. In the frosty mud she could still see the tracks of the transporter. The water in the hoofprints was frozen, and she put in a foot and gave a start when the thin ice cracked under her. Losing her balance, she nearly fell, but unexpectedly there was an arm there, a voice, the familiar smell of tobacco and hay, and for a moment she felt as if she were falling upwards. The steps creaked, and Herr Thamling carried her back to her bed and pulled the blanket up under her chin. Then he massaged her icy feet. 'Serbian for Beginners?' he asked with a shake of the head, looking at the bedside table. 'Why are you learning Serbian?'

And shortly afterwards the fever subsided, not by much, but it subsided, and her breathing became a little freer, she could see a bit more clearly and could already drink clear soup again or move a raisin back and forth in her mouth until it melted away. The man with the hat and the silver glasses came again, dropped a solution on her tongue and felt her pulse, looking around the room. 'Bovine typhus,' he said with a wink. 'You could be interesting to science, *kinderlach*. You are the first ever cow to read books.'

And after another week, after looking into the chamber pot, her mother stopped wearing overalls and rubber gloves. From now on her temperature was only taken under her armpits, and her mother left the door open so that her daughter could hear music, the radio in the kitchen, while she cooked her rice pudding or mashed potato with a little lemon juice stirred into it. As she cooked she said over and over again with a sigh how good and wise the old Jewish doctors were.

She too had recently grown sallow and thin, the rims of her eyelids looked inflamed and her face was shadowed with worries when she smiled. Once – Luisa had just woken from a long sleep – she stood smoking by the open window and stared absently into the courtyard, from which the sound of a lorry could be heard, a whistle and briskly shouted orders. In the evening sun traces of tears glistened on her cheeks, her hand trembled as she brushed a grey strand of hair behind her ear, and when Luisa asked her where her father and Billie were and why they hadn't come to see her, she threw the cigarette butt outside and walked over to the bed to straighten the covers. 'Oh, child,' she said, 'I've told you three times now! They're in Kiel, where else?'

Accordion music from somewhere, like honey that refuses to dissolve in water, and Luisa murmured: 'At the harbour?' Sinking into the plumped-up pillows she was about to ask whether the war was over; but then she fell asleep again.

*

187

The cows in the byre were uneasy and bellowed all day; the administrator couldn't yet allow them into the pasture. Russian planes were now seen more frequently, mostly one-engine Yaks which crossed the Baltic from Mecklenburg and shot at everything and everyone, even the trekking refugees. The straw and feed barns burned, and anyone who had to go from one village to another by bicycle or a car was advised to do so at night.

In the farmhouse too – in the Thamlings' flat, in the free attic rooms and in the drying loft – they were also putting up people who had been bombed or driven from their homes. Luisa stood in the corridor in her dressing gown and watched them bringing in their possessions: apart from the bags, baskets and feather beds they had a big wire cage of rabbits. They were visibly worn-out and exhausted people, and with them a smell came into the rooms that they knew from school: Goldgeist. Someone had lice.

From now on four women, an old man on crutches and three younger children shared the bathroom and toilet with them, and the kitchen was usually full and noisy; Luisa's mother only stayed there to cook. She had cleared the larder and the cupboards as far as possible and sat in the armchair in Sibylle's room, where she chopped fermented cherry leaves, a tobacco substitute, on a board. Or else she cut up pages from the magazines that were stacked around, pierced holes in the hand-sized pieces and bound them into wreaths with twine.

'Go back to bed,' she said one evening when Luisa came into the room, which was almost entirely dark. Only the heating element glowed. 'You're still weak, and who knows what these people are bringing with them. They're coming from the worst place.'

But her daughter slumped on the stool by the chest of drawers with the mirror on it, turned on the light and opened the little brass hook of the Handesgold cigar box. Almost all of her mop of hair lay under the lid with the two globes, and she added another handful of thin hairs from an envelope. Frau Thamling cut her remaining hair short, very short, so that it would recover; in the dressing-table mirror she looked like a dandelion. 'How do you know that Dad will come today?' she asked. 'Is there a working telephone in Kiel again?'

Her mother shook her head with a sigh, reached out her arm and pulled down the blackout blind. 'He's coming from Hamburg,' she said quietly. Her open dressing gown was already fraying at the seams, her pullover and sweat-pants were stained with milk and ash, and while she knotted the twine of a completed wreath Luisa looked at her furtively in the mirror. Her thin hands had blackish-blue veins, there were dark circles under her heavy-lidded eyes with their dried-up tear ducts, and her flabby cheeks drew down the corners of her mouth and made her colour-less lips look thinner than they were. She threw the wreath of toilet paper on the bed.

Her weary sadness tightened Luisa's throat, and she took a breath and said with forced cheerfulness: 'You know what, Mum? I'm not dreaming such terrible things any more, but since the fever I've been remembering all kinds of things from before. Particularly smells. My first doll smelled of oats, from the grass she was stuffed with, Dad's thumbs smelled of the newspaper, and when I'd spent a while sucking at the corner of the pillow it smelled like silver. I can even remember my baby days, the taste of your milk, imagine!'

Her mother started rolling a cigarette. 'Oh, really?' she asked and smiled faintly. 'What did that taste like?'

Luisa swallowed. 'I don't know,' she said, 'somehow bright and sweet.' Then she thought for a moment and waved her hand through the air. 'No, in fact it wasn't sweet at all. It had more of a . . . hint of almonds. But it also tasted a bit of nicotine. The flow was always far too thin to satisfy my hunger, my mouth really hurt from sucking, I remember very clearly! There was never enough. And then when I had whooping cough . . .'

She fell silent, because her eyes were suddenly filling with tears. With her hands in her lap she pushed down one of her cuticles and said in a low voice past the mirror: 'I'm sorry I worry you so much, Mama.'

A car horn sounded down below, and her mother raised her head. 'What was that? What makes you think such a thing, child? Worry isn't the word. It was almost impossible to reach you, and your imagination was running riot. Another week of temperatures like that, the doctor said, and you would have died on us!' She lit her hand-rolled cigarette from the electric heater and looked at the little box. 'Now look at your lovely hair! How that hurts me . . .'

The smoke from the cherry leaves had an acrid smell, like charred bread, but she still inhaled deeply. 'By the way I never breast-fed you, I was too old already. You had the bottle from day one,' she said. 'What's going on?'

The sound of heels rang out on the wooden floor, a voice with a sharp edge to it, and Luisa opened the door. The other refugees had stepped into the corridor or onto the stairs to the laundry room. A soldier in a wide motorcycle cape stood under the lamp and flicked with a twisted burn-scarred hand through a note pad. The cap that he wore was black, and what was clearly a new star gleamed on his collar. 'In case no one has told you, we are at war. Berlin is a frontline city, and you will have to adapt to circumstances,' he said, took a piece of chalk from the map pocket on his belt, tore off the paper wrapper and turned around. 'And now please stop that Jewish wailing! You're national comrades, aren't you?'

He had been talking to Luisa's father, and she didn't know what she was more afraid of: his appearance, or the chance that she might rush over to him in front of everybody, their expressions of curiosity and mockery. Her father was wearing a crumpled suit, but no tie; the end of it hung from his jacket pocket, and this evening, having only seen him clean shaven before, Luisa saw for the first time that his stubble was silvery grey, unlike his dark hair. His fingernails had never been so dirty either. 'If you will permit me, Scharführer, I am an admiral's steward,' he said, 'so not entirely without a military background. So there must have been some misunderstanding, isn't that so?'

The NCO clicked his tongue as if he had something between his teeth, left him standing there and wrote a few names on the doors of the room where they had previously lived; the chalk squeaked on the brown painted wood. 'The bombed-out people will be arriving tomorrow at noon,' he said. 'So we need room for another two women, three children and three war-wounded men. See to it that your personal objects disappear and leave heaters in the rooms. They are registered . . .'

Luisa's mother had stepped into the corridor as well and raised her eyebrows in mute enquiry. Open-mouthed she stared at the names on the sitting-room door and above Billie's photograph of Zarah Leander, presented her palms and asked hoarsely: 'Yes, has that been agreed with the owner of the farm? I can hardly believe it. Hauptsturmführer Landes is our son-in-law. There are four of us in the family. Where, excuse me, are we supposed to live?'

The man put the pad in his map bag and pointed to Luisa's open room: 'As I said, no beds or straw sacks are to go in there. Just huddle up, and be glad that you've got a solid roof over your heads. Do you think you're the only ones who are under pressure these days?'

But Luisa's father, after a quick glance at his wife, raised a finger and swung it in the air like a pendulum. 'No, no, that's impossible,' he insisted. 'I will record my objection, Scharführer. My daughter has until recently been seriously ill. She can't live with several people in a tiny room, not least for reasons of hygiene. She needs rest and recuperation.'

The NCO pulled on his gloves. 'Right,' he murmured and studied Luisa, 'who couldn't use a bit of that these days?'

Only half as old as her father, late twenties at most, he was a head taller, and was suddenly standing so close to him that the tips of their shoes touched. Standing like that so he wrinkled his nose, as if he smelled something bad. 'What is an admiral's steward, by the way? It's nothing but a waiter or a messenger-boy, isn't that right?' He barely moved his lips, but spat the words so audibly through his teeth that everyone in the corridor could hear him. 'So we've got someone who's poured some gravy, cleaned a few ashtrays and glugged down the leftovers from the glasses – and in all seriousness he wants to query an order?'

Luisa's father didn't seem to be breathing, his face looked waxen and his eyes bulged slightly. His stubbly Adam's apple twitched, and the officer clapped him gently on the shoulder, closed his eyelids for a moment and said: 'Oh, no, I don't think so. You're too clever for that, aren't you; you have a family, after all. Have a nice evening everybody, Sieg Heil!' He fastened the poppers on his gloves, a delicate click on his wrists, and walked to the door. But on the threshold he turned around once again and asked, 'Who was that, by the way? Isn't there another daughter? Another redhead?'

Luisa thought she could hear a curious undertone in the question, something amused or even frivolous, and she looked at her parents, although they remained silent. With both hands on the collar of her dressing gown – she wrapped the fabric around her fingers – her mother drew her lips inwards and closed her quivering eyelids. She sank against her husband, who put an arm around her shoulders and stared at the floor, the bruised roses with the nail-heads pushing through. And Luisa said for her: 'My sister is in Kiel!'

The officer, with both thumbs behind his belt, studied

the parents before nodding. 'Oh really? Well then . . .' Grinning, he walked to the stairwell, where the light didn't work; but the moonlight falling through the round window made the death's-head on his cap shine. 'That means we've got one more bed.'

*

When she came back from fetching the milk the next morning, her father was already awake. His hair was tousled, the bald spot on the back of his head was exposed. His T-shirt, previously white, was stained, and his braces hung from his waistband. Holding a bottle of red wine in one hand, he rummaged with the other in the cutlery drawer. 'Good morning!' she said. 'Did you sleep well? I've brought you the fresh quark that you like so much. There are cherries as well.'

Her blue-bound volume of Gryphius poems lay on the table, and he smiled wearily and swallowed hard; a pomaded strand of hair fell into his forehead. 'Thanks, my darling, that's sweet of you. If there's anything I've missed recently it was that quark.' Then he opened another drawer. 'But right now what I could use is a corkscrew . . .'

She put the jug down on the cold stove and unwound her scarf from her neck. 'It's in the sitting room, in the cupboard,' she said and walked across the corridor. The room was still in darkness, and when she turned on the light she noticed the blankets and the dented hot-water bottle on the couch. Her father's shirt and jacket hung on a chair, his tie on the tusk of the boar's head on the wall, and back in the kitchen she asked as casually as she could manage: 'Didn't you sleep with Mama?'

The bedroom, little more than an alcove, was separated from the sitting room by a sliding door, and he raised one shoulder in an apparent gesture of regret and sat down at the table. 'I wanted to,' he replied and opened the wine and sniffed the cork. 'I really wanted to, in fact, but unfortunately she threw me out. I think it was because I was snoring.'

With the key that she carried on a little string around her neck, Luisa opened the cupboard. 'Why?' she asked and handed him a water glass. 'You always snore!'

He filled it almost to the brim. 'Is that true? Well, maybe,' he replied. 'But last night it was probably in the wrong key. By the way, you'll have heard: we're going to have to huddle up a bit closer. That is, you take Mama with you into your book cave, and I'll be in Kiel most of the time anyway. You'll manage. And if I have to stay away for longer, please don't worry, do you hear me? You'll always be kept well supplied, Klaas promised me.'

He drank the wine as if it was water, and Luisa sat down next to him, spooned some of the quark into a little bowl and stirred in a few cherries. As she did she scanned the poem that he was holding open in the book, and asked, 'Why will you be away for longer?'

His stubble crackled as he rubbed his chin. 'You're right, there's no sensible reason,' he said. 'But first of all the roads are getting worse, you can hardly get out of the city. And secondly: when I recall that gentleman from last night, I'm almost afraid that neither he nor his playmates need sensible reasons.' He put his hand on the back of her neck and kissed her forehead. 'Oh, I'm so pleased that you're better.'

He filled his glass again, and Luisa ate the quark, spat out a cherry stone and asked, 'Why is Billie actually in Kiel? Is it because of me? Or is she helping you in the canteen? Mama said . . .'

'What?' he interrupted her. 'Why because of you?'

'Well . . . Because I'd have infected her?'

He nodded thoughtfully and sniffed the wine. As always when he drank alcohol before breakfast, his voice darkened after only a few sips, and the words, as if a sediment were making them heavier, emerged more slowly from his lips. 'That's exactly it,' he said. 'Frau Thamling and your mother had already had typhus, they're immune and were able to look after you. But your sister . . . You shouldn't risk something like that.'

A bluish weariness surrounded his eyes as he studied the pregnant woman who had come into the kitchen without a word of greeting. There was a Mother's Cross on the man's jacket that she wore and, clearly annoyed that no one had lit the fire, she clattered the rings on the oven and shovelled ashes from the stove. A cloud of dust rose from the bucket. Luisa put the lid on the cherry jar. 'Are the bombs still falling on Kiel?'

Again he drained his wine, some of it dripping on his vest, got to his feet and picked up the bottle from the table. 'Not at all,' he said, already standing in the doorway. 'There's nothing left to destroy.'

*

The sun shone and the ditches steamed. Prisoners in striped canvas uniforms repaired the road. Guarded by Volkssturm men, they shovelled gravel into the shell-holes and stamped it down. Others boiled tar in metal vats and poured it over the gravel, some of it seeping here and there into the grass, over coltsfoot, clover and veronica. They were all shaven-headed and nothing but skin and bone, and they stepped mutely aside when she pushed her bicycle around the black holes.

The village street was undamaged, chickens pecked moss from the cracks between the cobbles, and for a moment Luisa paused and listened. The wind blew over the edges of the thatched roofs, the hollow stems whistled and buzzed as if the silence were being combed. She knocked at the kitchen door and the lace curtains fluttered as she opened it. Ole was sitting at the table, painting snail shells and seashells, and he smiled at her. 'You look like a boy,' he said. 'I like it. Are you better?'

Luisa nodded. 'I was never ill, if you want to know the truth. I just pretended to be so that they'd leave me in peace. No one at home?'

He bit into a piece of sugar bread and said with his mouth full: 'Grandpa's with the Gauleiter setting up tank traps, and Mama is collecting hair. She'll be back soon.'

She sat down beside him. 'Why? Where's she getting it from?'

He jutted his lower lip and shrugged. 'No idea. What's that you've got there? A present?'

'Yes,' Luisa said, 'but not for you, you greedy thing.

You've just had one.' She pointed to the brightly coloured shells beside his paint box. 'Have you been to the seaside?'

'No,' the boy said, 'we're not allowed to go to the beach any more because of the mines. I found the shells digging on the other side of the duck pond. Just imagine, the little convent lake in the forest was once enormous and deep, about a thousand years ago. The water reached all the way to Bovenau, Grandpa said, and there were probably pirates, sea-snakes and fire-breathing dragons here. Do you believe that too?'

'Of course,' Luisa said. 'There still are. Look at your own fish-face.'

He laughed, and she walked through the glass door into his mother's working area and set the cigarette box down on the big table. Bowl-shaped lamps hung above it, and a dozen or so model heads in wood or leather were lined up on the edge. Covered with flesh-coloured tulle and wreathed in hairpins, they wore wigs – just begun, half completed or nearly finished – for women and men in many different colours and sizes. There was even a bright blond one for a child.

Combs, scissors and brushes hung from a board on the wall, and in one of those flat boxes meant for eels and smoked fish from the fish market there were braids of various lengths and different kinds of plait. Almost all of them were black or dark brown and Ole, who was leaning in the doorway, said: 'Mama has had to work a lot recently, her eyes are always streaming. But the people in the city have burns from phosphorus bombs; their hair doesn't grow any more. She has orders for five years, it takes hundreds of thousands of stitches per wig, and I might even get a bigger bike. I'd like a Sekura, with the clover leaf on the bell, you know the one?'

Luisa lifted one of the shiny black braids. It was surprisingly heavy and as thick as her wrist where the hair had been removed. The cut surface looked very uneven, as if the scissors or the knife had been blunt, and rusty too, and at the pointed end it was held together by a rubber band with a Bakelite brooch, a ladybird that now had hardly any paint on it. She put it back carefully.

'I thought *Emil and the Detectives* was exciting, by the way,' Ole said. 'Thank you very much! My favourite was Pony Hütchen, she reminded me of you. But Herr Milger, the man in charge of our block, took it off me before I'd finished. He says Emil Tischbein is a Jew, you can tell by the name, and because he pins money to the lining of his jacket with a safety pin.' He curiously opened the Handelsgold box and studied the contents. 'And they've banned the book in Berlin – is that true?'

Luisa, blinking into the sunlight, didn't reply. She walked past the model heads, pushed a stool aside and approached a work bench below the window. There was a kind of loom on it, about fifty centimetres square, strung with some lengths of cord. Blond strands hung from it like tresses and stirred faintly in the draught. 'That's my grandpa's working place,' the boy said. 'He doesn't see very well any more, and Mama only lets him weave. That's what you call it when you thread short hairs. Don't touch, he'll notice straight away!'

All the scissors, brushes and weaving needles on the

table lay side by side at right angles to the table edge, arranged by size. A panel showing different shades hung on the wall, and standing on the windowsill, overshadowed by a plant with whitish buds, were two model heads. The one made of scuffed leather, whose seam ran over its forehead, nose and chin, was only covered by a tulle mount, while on the one next to it, a wooden one which bore the suggestion of a face with striking eyebrows and cheekbones, there was a wig, but it still lacked some stitches. An area above the ear was bald.

Growth rings and branch eyes were just visible through the very thin gauze. Stepping up to the edge of the table, Luisa reached out an arm, touched the softly waving hair and gave a start; in her imagination it should have been cold. It was densely woven and felt powerful, although perhaps a little faded by the sun and, amazed at how many colours there were in a single shock of hair, she rubbed the tips between her fingers for a moment. Then she moved a lock from the wooden forehead, which was branded with a number: 41978.

She carefully lifted the head from the window ledge: possibly hollow, it was so unexpectedly light that for a moment she lost her balance and had to regain her footing on the brick floor. And no sooner had she blown a downy feather and a tiny dead fly from the skull and, through the initial smell of dust, caught the almost faded odour that seemed to drift to her from a long way away, than her chin began to tremble and the sunlight blurred in her eyes. A cock crowed behind the cracked pane.

'Mama put that head aside,' Ole said, taking a card

game out of his pocket. 'There's hardly any demand for red, you know. I'm sure she'll be delighted about your hair, she'll be able to fill up that bald patch, but most people want blond or dark wigs, they're the ones that bring in money.' He started shuffling and smiled at her. 'Shall we play Mau-Mau?'

*

There were no aeroplanes far and wide; but she still cycled along the beaten path beside the bumpy cobbles, and not only because it was more comfortable. As soon as a low-flying plane appeared, you could quickly dip down into the ditch, among the undergrowth. A wind surged in from the Baltic, last year's rosehips skipped down the road, and sometimes she had to turn her head to be able to breathe. She was drenched in sweat beneath her inflated anorak.

The old bicycle creaked and rattled, and when a gust of wind caught her from the side she had difficulty maintaining her direction; she sank against the embankment and lay for a while in the saltmarsh grass, staring at the fleeing clouds. Pale pink blossoms, ragged birds' nests and egg-shells whirled around, and in spite of the roaring wind the sound of piercing cries could be heard, as if birds were calling to their young.

The streams of water in the springs and troughs along the roadside blew over the edge of the basins, and in order to avoid the approaching storm she turned off the Kiel Road and took a detour via Quarnbek and Ottendorf. The closer she got to the city, the more lorries or tanks lay in the ditches and fields, among the germinating seeds.

Shredded tarpaulins fluttered and flapped, gusts of wind whistled in the gun barrels and the smoke from the vehicles smelled of diesel and burnt flesh.

At about midday the storm subsided a little. Even so, she didn't make better progress; the streets towards the centre of the city, narrowed by the ravaged tram-tracks or the rubble of the fallen houses, were merely bumpy paths, and where people with suitcases, bags or prams came towards her she had to get off and push her bicycle into the debris to make room.

In the shattered doorway of Schramm's Hotel, a poster still hung: a big skeleton sat astride a Halifax plane, throwing bombs with its bony hands. 'Lights out!' it said underneath. 'The enemy can see your light!' All three floors were burnt out, charred remains of curtains flapped from the empty window frames, and the hinges squeaked when the wind stirred the crooked shutters.

Even the southern cemetery had been hit. Planks protruded from the churned-up graves, scraps of fabric hanging from them; the Kapellenberg was burning. Sulphurous smoke billowed from the central station, the ribs of the dome, and the wharves on the eastern shore of the Förde seemed to have been entirely destroyed. The formerly mighty cranes, which had looked like spread-legged monsters, lay bent or toppled, the docks were bombed to pieces and ships lay bottom-up in the water. Sticky black birds swam among the flickering lakes of phosphorus, powerlessly flapping their wings.

Luisa cycled over the dyke, past the ruin of Kiel Castle. Behind it the view was free to Holtenauer Strasse and St

Paul's Church on Niemannsweg, because the old city, once densely built, had been completely demolished. Beneath the reddish-brown field of bricks, beneath its cloud of dust, from which a few charred beams and a piece of fire-wall protruded, one could see the shapes of the hills that had been here in prehistoric times, before the area was inhabited. Rats darted about on it.

In the rubble of the villas on the Krusenkoppel, armed men kept watch to deter looters, and everywhere people in striped uniforms were busy smashing up concrete blocks and carting away rubble. The Kiellinie, the path along the Förde, had already been cleared and shoes, spectacles and the handle of a briefcase lay in the tarmac, which had melted and hardened again. The building of Beuker the stationer's was in ruins, and the 'Geha' insurance advertisements were hidden behind white dust. Fat seagulls squatted along Brandenburger Strasse and flew wearily up from the quay wall as Luisa approached.

As she pushed her heavy bicycle up Langer Kram, sailors came towards her, a U-boat crew. Clearly drunk – their eyes were glazed and their steps, despite their efforts, uncertain – the eight men looked serious and concentrated and didn't say a word. Their cap bands fluttered in the wind that blew their collars up into the back of their necks, and only one of them paid any attention to Luisa. He waved to her, before he and his comrades climbed into the shaft by the quay which led to the boats anchored below ground level, and she waved wearily back.

Apart from the burnt-out gatehouse, the two-storey brick buildings of the barracks were undamaged, as her father had said. The passenger vehicles and transporters in the internal courtyard were uncamouflaged, and the nets lay by the coolers. There were no guards to be seen, and clearly the caretaker had stopped scrubbing the swastika over the entrance to the canteen; the granite was white with pigeon droppings. Laughter echoed from the mezzanine floor, uniformed men crowded behind the murky windows, and Luisa rested her bicycle against the wall and climbed the three steps to the door all at once.

But with such painful calves that last effort was probably too much for her still diminished strength. Staggering, she clung tightly to the railings, and one of the Russian cleaning-women who was just coming out of the building looked at her in amazement. 'What's up, *devochka*?' she asked and touched her cheeks, dabbing the sweat from her forehead with the sleeve of her overall. 'You ill? Itler finished?'

Tethered to the radiator, two dogs slept in the corridor, and the view inside the smoke-filled mess was scarcely less murky than it was from the outside, since the windows were painted with splinter-proof protective varnish. Below the arched ceiling with the huge chandelier, which was made to look like a ship's wheel, a gang of soldiers were roaring along with the tune played by an accordionist in a wheelchair: 'Back where the lighthouse stands'. There were also civilians sitting at the tables, some in leather coats, and corporals and lance corporals stood in a crowd several rows deep, waving banknotes in the air and calling out their orders.

There was a cordon in front of the stairs to the officers'

mess on the first floor. The buffet, behind whose curved glass there would normally have been gherkins, meatballs and boxes full of sprats, was empty, and Luisa pushed her way among the young men and slipped through the swing door. Four members of staff were working behind the counter, women in light-blue aprons with pointed bonnets wedged in their hair, but the only one she knew was Elisabeth. She was standing at the bar, holding one glass after another under the flowing stream of beer, without touching the tap at all. She was also smoking a cigarette. 'Luisa?' she called over her shoulder. 'What are you doing here? Has something happened? Just a second . . .'

Another woman was passing her the brand-new tulip glasses straight from the box, and after a good two dozen were half-full Elisabeth pushed them back one row at a time. Only then did she turn off the beer tap, dried her hands and came out from behind the bar. From one of the many old constantly dripping lead-lined ice-boxes she produced a Molke lemonade and snapped the cap open. 'Thank you!' Luisa said and drank. 'Do you know where my sister is?'

Elisabeth dropped her cigarette end and stubbed it out with her toe. 'My goodness, I don't believe it!' she said, looking at the metal clips on her trousers. 'Have you cycled the whole way from the farm? Have you lost your mind? You were seriously ill!'

She too felt her forehead and drew one of her eyelids down with her thumb, and Luisa drank again, set the bottle down and insisted, 'But now I'm well. So tell me: where is Billie? Mama and Papa said she was in Kiel . . . They've said that several times. Does she work here?' She pointed to the stairs. 'Does she live with you in the attic?'

Elisabeth looked into the crowd, from which someone had called her name, nodded and unscrewed the top of a schnapps bottle. 'Listen . . .' she said and they both pressed themselves against the counter to make room for a waitress. 'You can see what's going on here. They're all poor wretches who are about to face the guns and want to be served quickly – which you can understand, can't you? Go to the kitchen and get them to give you something to eat or lie down in my room upstairs and have a rest. You'll find chocolate in the cupboard. I get a break in an hour, then I'll come and see you and we can talk quietly.'

She inserted a nozzle with a tiny flapping cap into the bottle, and when Luisa didn't reply, but just looked at her with stinging eyes, she added in a lower voice: 'Walter has already been taken prisoner, just imagine. Luckily by the Americans, somewhere in Bavaria. So he doesn't have to go to Siberia and can marry me if he's still keen . . . But I'm not at all sure that he deserves me. He's sent me nothing from his war, not a necklace, not a scarf, not so much as a jar of jam. Never have anything to do with boys!'

Avoiding Luisa's eye, she stepped to the shelf, put all her fingers in ten shot glasses – which enlarged her fingertips like a magnifying glass – and set them down on a small tray. Then she waggled the nozzle over them, filled them beyond the calibration mark with schnapps and sighed: 'Oh, come, child, don't make things so hard for yourself! I can't tell you anything. Your parents need to do that. I'm only employed here, and your father will throw me out, if

I . . . And I passed on your greetings to Walter, I was allowed to do that, wasn't I?'

She held the tray out into the roaring crowd and raked in a few coins with the edge of her hand. As she did so she gnawed her lip, and at last she bent down and muttered: 'It'll soon all be over! More and more officers are taking to their heels, the mess up at the top is a tragedy. And your Billie will get through it all, I firmly believe it. Such a strong woman . . . They've stopped just killing people in the camps, they can't afford to do it any more; they need them to work here. Look at the streets: all the rubble, people buried alive . . . The whole of Kiel is being cleared by prisoners and forced labourers.'

The accordion fell silent and the girl opened her mouth without managing to get a word out. Somewhere in the noise glass clinked, dogs barked, and a sailor leaned over the bar, a young U-boat corporal, and waved a fan of bank-notes around. His hair and eyebrows bright blond, his cheeks red, he called out: 'Champagne! I want to drink champagne again! Give me a big bottle of your best, boss, Napoleon or something! Don't worry about glasses.'

Elisabeth stroked Luisa's back, pushed her gently aside and turned to the drunk. 'Oh, young man,' she said sadly. 'Do you know how much it costs? Save your money! Buy your girlfriend something nice and have a beer.'

But the sailor, who had very pale blue eyes and no hair on his chin, and from whose shirt a silver cross dangled, waved his hand dismissively and lowered his eyes. He ran his thumb through a puddle on the counter. 'What use is money to me now,' he said. 'We're not coming back anyway.'

The evening sun shone through the chinks between the planks of the open barn on the country road to Quarnbek. Almost twenty men were lying on camp beds or sheaves of straw and looked at her. Their eyes were open wide or half-closed with exhaustion, their cheeks pale and sunken above their full beards, and their clothes were so dirty and ragged that it was only on closer inspection that they were recognizable as uniforms: Russian. Some prisoners wore boots, but most of them only foot-rags, and each had a cannula with a tube in his bare arm.

A soldier of the Waffen-SS and a nurse walked around among the rows and examined the vacuum flasks beside the camp beds. They were filling up drop by drop with the blood of the men, who were guarded by several members of the Hitler Youth wearing knee-length trousers. They carried new sub-machine guns on their shoulder belts, and when one of them hissed at her and jerked his pelvis obscenely, Luisa pedalled away.

She cycled along the canal for a while. On the opposite bank a row of fishing rods was wedged in the ground; the bells tinkled and the water foamed white where U-boats glided below the surface towards the North Sea. The light was fading, the ferry house and the window of the convent were already in darkness. A flock of thrushes fluttered up from the garden when a big Mercedes drove past it at great speed. The driver looked severely out from under the rim of his steel helmet.

On the back seat two officers sat flicking through files,

and in spite of his uniform and cap Luisa recognized one of them as the man from Vinzent's birthday party. The reflection of the orange sky slid across the lenses of his glasses when he looked at her and even turned his head slightly so that she could see his scar, the proud flesh, and then the car had already reached the canal, and the grains of sand whirled up as it passed and scratched her mud-guards, her face. Before it reached the ferry building the car turned off towards Rendsburg.

From a distance she heard the lowing of the cows on the farm; the evening milking had begun. A light bulb flick-ered in the open churn room but there was no one in the yard as she cycled over the bridge. Motte, sitting between the pillars in the porch of the big house, wagged his tail, and Luisa got off her bicycle and scratched his fur, so that he whimpered and snuggled up to her. Sirens sounded in the distance, and a short while later bombers flew past the farm heading south, perhaps to Neustadt or Itzehoe. Someone closed the door of the byre.

Now it was almost dark under the linden tree, only a few white narcissi pierced the darkness in the front garden, and she pushed her bicycle to the barn. A chicken flapped towards her out of the half-open door and darted off to the side before it disappeared cackling into the field. There was no light in the building, which held an old tractor with steel wheels, a grain binder and her father's bucket car. By day some light fell through the loopholes above the hayloft, now the wind whistled through them, and Luisa leaned exhaustedly against the wall.

Her legs hurt. The double-walled churns in the byre

rang out like gongs, and children squealed behind the barn. The big storage boxes beside the gate had been empty for a long time but still smelled of the previous year's apples and pears, and from somewhere came the sound of whispering and rustling, and something that sounded like tiny feet pattering on metal. But she kept her painful eyelids closed. Her throat was so dry from her long ride through the Baltic wind that she could hardly swallow. Her lips tasted salty.

It was only when she heard a clatter in the hay barn that she looked up. The board walls, the storerooms full of firewood and peat for the stove, and the black silhouettes of the machines impeded any kind of vision, but in spite of the darkness she felt no fear – which had less to do with her exhaustion, her sad drowsiness, and more with the arrival of a comforting aroma. The smell of winter fruit, tyre rubber and tractor oil beneath the high roof mingled suddenly with the elegant scent of pine trees, witch hazel and a hint of menthol, and she raised her chin and called out quietly: 'Dad?'

A bat fluttered close to her ear. Spider webs brushed her cheeks and hands as she felt her way between a dented water-tank on wheels and the car with the fabric roof. The space was cramped, and she accidentally bumped against the front fender, much wider than the rear one, and rubbed her knee with a groan. Then she reached in through the open window for the quartz keyring, and carefully turned the key in the lock. After a moment's hesitation the headlights came on.

Insects were already tumbling through the faint light,

and as soon as she saw the dust floating in the air she couldn't help coughing. The stalks of hay on the winch of the grain-binder had a golden gleam when the draught caught them. At first it was impossible to see what was beam and what shadow below the hayloft with the cross-shaped slits in the wall, but she could now sense a mute presence. A ladder with missing rungs lay on the mud floor, the axe was still stuck in an up-ended chopping block, a massive oak-tree trunk, and in the middle of the two white lines that shone from the blackout hoods of the headlights and struck the wall, the tarred bricks, she recognized his silhouette.

A sudden pulse in her throat, and horror to the roots of her hair was followed by a confusion that made her feel dizzy for a moment: the fact that she wasn't breathless, that she didn't lose her composure, didn't tremble or cry or run screaming away seemed to her both proof that this sight wasn't real and that there could be no doubt. She stepped into his shadow, stepped unexpectedly on the tie that lay there and tried to make out his face above her. And in the end it didn't matter whether she cried out or only imagined that she had.

His answer, or what she perceived as his answer, came out of the infinity between two heartbeats: although the farm still echoed with the lowing of the cows in the byre opposite, the cries of the women and the laughter of the children as they sent jets of milk shooting from the teats into each other's mouths, her father was surrounded by his own profoundly serious silence. Beneath its weight the darkness around her seemed to condense once more, and she felt clearly that it was the actual meaning, the secret heart of the word 'death'. When she reached into the slits and pulled the rubber hoods from the headlights, the ploughshares in the corner flashed like a row of silver teeth.

To look at him more closely, she involuntarily adopted the same posture, head tilted, as the hanged man. His collar was crumpled on the inside, the skin around the rope was blue, and when she thought about it later, it was never his freshly shaven, fragrant cheeks or the shadows around his tightly closed eyes that struck her first, it was never the bitter-looking narrow-lipped grin or the big urine stain on his trousers, it wasn't the shoe that dangled from his foot, revealing a torn sock. What she always thought of first was the position of his swollen hands with their cleaned nails and the first liver spots, their backs towards the front, making the elbows stand out slightly. He had never held his arms like that in life.

'The universe is weightless,' Herr Thamling used to say when someone's burden was too heavy for them, and now she understood those words. The hayloft creaked again and she carefully pulled the dead man's shoe over his heel. Then she reached up and held his fingers, which were cool but not yet cold, and ran her thumb over the back of his hand. His wedding ring had embedded itself deep in his skin; the second hand on his watch jerked forward and she even thought she could hear it ticking. But perhaps again that was the little feet on the metal roof. She pushed the door shut and ran across the yard.

Children were playing in the corridor of the farmhouse too. They crouched on the steps folding paper aeroplanes or cutting brownish figures and objects from old catalogues. Washing over the banisters and from the tips of the antlers on the wall; radio music and laughter came from the kitchen in the attic, and Luisa pushed open the door to her room. Warm air rushed towards her: the element in the heater was glowing.

With Billie's dressing gown over her knees, her mother sat on the edge of the bed smoking. Her favourite cup, the one with the pattern of violets that had recently lost its handle, stood on her bedside table, a bottle of schnapps beside her, and Luisa took a deep breath and called softly, because she didn't want the other refugees to hear her: 'Mama, Mama, come quickly!' And only now did her voice blur with tears. 'Papa has hanged himself!'

But her mother didn't react, she just smeared ash onto a saucer. The hairs on the back of her head had thinned from lying down so much, and she took a sip before looking around at her daughter. Her grey eyes were weary, as if she were looking through dust. 'Again?' she murmured at last, barely moving her lips, and when she shook her head the slack skin under her chin wobbled. She drew on her cigarette. 'Well, then leave him hanging for a while, I would say. And make sure he's really dead.'

Perhaps, once the lake withdraws, it will come to light: being granted the vision of a work is by no means the same as having the strength and the fortune of circumstances to bring it to completion. Everything is in the hands of the Lord, just as we are flayed and broken on the wheel. We are left with the incomprehension that he bestows on everyone like a fish seeing a coin. We are left with the vague hope that our life will have a meaning with him at least, even a golden one, though the zealous work may lie shattered like a chamber pot in the mud.

Between evening and morning, war – the work of the Devil with his partnering of saltpetre and sulphur – returned to our forests. Smoke drifted over the lake upon which floated the church, our heart's little chapel. And even if the clash of the armies beyond the Ochsenweg was not meant for us, it was the height of stupidity to let the cattle go on grazing in the pastures, however pointed their horns or bone-crushing their hooves. They went to the knife and were devoured by those who could not keep pace with the camp followers, whether because of injury or strong drink.

The back-and-forth bullets of the field and chamber,

singer and nightingale by name, whistled over our thatched roofs and hissed into the lake, and the horses perished and left us alone with our depleted strength. And the people, long weary of fighting, crept back among the thorny thickets, where there were no paths for the villains and their pikes. And so the two old men were left alone in the village with their illusion, namely the author of this chronicle Bredelin Merxheim, and his companion Johann Bubenleb.

Hand's breadth by hand's breadth we approached our goal, the finely carved wisdom of Horace could already be read in the arch above the door. The wind, which stirred the flames from the embers, dried our eyes, our soft spines cracked, and still we put our all in, because what else was there to do in those days? It was only when the scattered soldiers came to the village, marauders weighed down with weapons, that the work had to rest and a hiding place be swiftly found for the night. Devotees of Bacchus all, they brought lust and intoxication into our huts and made off in the morning in pursuit of the next death, in many cases their own. May God forgive their stinking souls.

And soon after it happened: the chapel, which we thought was already at the shore, listed on the capricious waves and drifted off course. A storm came up, thunder and lightning crashed down with a rain riddled with sharp hailstones whose like no one could remember seeing. Clothes clung icily to bodies, hat-brims drooped and to make matters worse one of the rotten cables on the boat was torn and could not be mended without entering the raging waves. But no one could swim, so all would have drowned.

So we pulled the frisky church on a rope, and grim-faced Bubenleb shouted through the storm: how did he spin all this together on his sheet of paper, when it should have been left virgin white? What else, old Merxheim, is due to come in this summer of comets? All we need is for stray cannon-fire to come our way! But then it will be *gut's Nächtle*, good night, as my wife, the wise Swabian, used to say!

Beneath his rough talk he was, as I have explained already, hewn from the finest timber, and his grimness was inspired by goodness; so he needed no reply. 'Speak of . . .' his inkpot-wielding companion from the inkpot groaned and braced himself more firmly against the storm, his feet clawing more deeply into the mud: 'Speak of the Devil and he . . .' But who can doubt the power of the word once thought, and the Devil was already crashing into the wall – not of the church, but of the boat that had been built with such care, and which immediately filled with water.

We humans stood frozen and aslant, and even the goats, with wet shore grass in their mouths, stared startled. A smoking cannonball it was, black with powder, the size of a fallen angel, and in an instant the lake engulfed a dream leaving nothing, not so much as the tip of the tower. The rush and murmur of the waves in the reeds sounded like mischievous laughter.

O old eyes, wide with disbelief! Ruined we were, utterly. O gouty hands, too weak for prayer! We pulled our hats down before the void. As the noise of battle vanished north-wards, probably towards Denmark, and corpse-robbers and mercy-killers swarmed over the fields in search of lucre, bent-backed with sorrow we went to the house of Johann Bubenleb, to warm our feet by the fire. And then, over punch from a clay beaker, tears came once more to the eyes of the author of this chronicle, the bitterest tears now, and he no longer knew what he was living for.

But the craftsman, once he had refilled his cup, grinned with all his gappy teeth. He cut a piece of blue sheep's cheese, put it on the bread and said with his mouth full: I think I can already hear from the bottom of the lake, my dear Bredelin, the hiccup of the bell! Hic-hoc! The well-read current turns the Bible pages, psalm such-and-such, and the winged angels intoning their round-mouthed Hallelujah gurgle most beautifully along with the organ!

Most likely he meant the wind that whistled through the cracks of his hut, octaves of derision, and when his interlocutor had no words to utter in reply and only stared into the hole of the stove, his friend rested his hand on his neck and continued gravely: Why then must he blow affliction over the days of his old age! Master Merxheim! Must a bent nail point you in the right direction? What in truth has been lost? This was not a wash-house, or a shit-house for that matter, it was not a sty for pigs, was it?

We sit freely at the centre beneath the celestial arch, and while the God of this summer may despise our nearness – can he remove himself further than the thought intended for him? Have we not tried everything within the realm of human possibility? Our drudgery, for which no one earned as much as a pfennig, is hardly to be doubted; every fibre of our aching backs bears witness to us. Our efforts were pure and perfect, and could not have been truer, so everything has been successful, my Bredelin: seen by the Lord's light we have reached our goal. The little church is in its rightful place! Think on that!

In the midday silence the only sound was the treadmill, the butter-dog in the dairy. Luisa waited by the new spruce-wood stairs leading up to the milkers' rooms. A row of rubber boots stood on the platform, new amber tears sparkled in the sun here and there, and Walter grinned wearily and nodded to her.

He wore a khaki-coloured blouson with epaulettes, tight trousers with patch pockets and ankle-high laced boots. With a few shirts and the red velvet cover from his bed over his arm, he tramped down the last few steps, came to a stop beside the motorbike and looked at her affably. 'Hey, you? How are those big fat tomes of yours?' he said. 'They've still got all their letters in there?'

With her arms folded over her chest, she smiled vaguely and ran the tip of her shoe through the aromatic sawdust on the floor. Even though she had only recently rearranged her books, alphabetically by author, she felt as if he were asking about a different, far-off time; she had read very little for months. She quickly studied him from top to toe and was relieved to see no scars or bandages. But he was paler now, and much thinner too, and his posture expressed a weariness that belied his age.

There was a sandy glow on his cheeks. When he had arrived an hour before on the loudly rattling motorbike, passing by the duck pond on his way to the big house after calling in at the byre, she had quickly changed her clothes: she was wearing Sibylle's suede pumps, her midnight-blue dress and the little necklace with the single pearl. But he didn't seem to notice. He smiled and said, 'Wasn't your hair longer before?'

There was a new expression in his eyes, a different seriousness with an underlying melancholy, but perhaps it only seemed that way to her because of his prominent cheekbones, or because the shadow of the flag darkened his face. His beautiful mouth with its almost feminine outline seemed thinner to her, more colourless than before, and she brushed her strands of hair, which had grown strongly back, behind her ear and answered: 'It's been shorter too.'

He nodded, his eyelids closed, and seemed to understand. He threw the things into the motorcycle sidecar to join a suitcase, a cardboard box full of papers and steel-tipped work boots. 'Your Karl May's in good shape. Oh, and sorry about your father, by the way. Terrible thing. I barely knew him, but I think he was a good man. He had a nice face. Was there a farewell note? Do you know why he did it?'

Luisa shook her head quickly and rubbed her upper arms as if she were shivering. More and more unsettled by the fact that he seemed to have no sense of the urgency of the moment, she didn't want to talk to him about the past, not about the calf or about her father. As she looked at the faint dip in his chin, she already thought she could feel the stubble under her fingers. 'Who says he did it?' she replied and smiled quickly so as not to leave too much room for his puzzlement. 'What kind of uniform is that?'

Frowning, he looked down at himself and shrugged. The patches under his armpits had white edges. 'Well, it's American,' he replied. 'It says here: US Army. And here, Private Fitzgerald, that's the owner's name. They gave it to me in prison in Dachau, because I was wearing only rags.' He raised a foot. 'But these boots are the best thing. I've traipsed through the whole country in them. They're indestructible.'

He was already playing with his motorcycle key; she nodded with apparent interest and, panicking, wondered what she had left to say or ask, she felt so stupid. But all of a sudden he extended his arm and took her hand, which vanished almost entirely in his. She felt something like an electric shock in the backs of her knees and she couldn't breathe, but he held her at a distance: he separated out one finger, inevitably the index finger with the trace of nail varnish that she had tried out days before, and poked it into a tiny hole in the jacket. 'This is where the bullet got him.'

Right next to the breast pocket, precisely level with the heart, and she gave a start and tried to draw back – but how could she get so close to him again? She had also dabbed two drops from one of her sister's perfume bottles under her armpits, a faint scent of musk and honey, which she hoped would make her seem a little older, and she swallowed hard before she said, 'Herr Thamling had to fire you, didn't he?'

Walter nodded towards the flagpole in the middle of the

yard, the Union Jack. 'Yes, that's how our new masters want it,' he replied. 'Soon everything here will be done mechanically, even insemination and calving. No one's going to need trained milkers, just unskilled workers and engineers. I've got another job from next week, up near Schleswig, I'll probably be a foreman. You can visit me there if you get a holiday.'

She took a deep breath but then didn't dare say what was on the tip of her tongue. The dress, made of a smooth cotton fabric, was tighter across her breasts when she straightened her back, she had tried that out by the mirror, and she tottered slightly on her unfamiliar heels, while responding to his smile with a defiant glance. Her sweat tickled as it ran between her shoulder blades.

Walter was no longer gripping her hand; even so, she left her finger in the hole in his blouson. The green of his iris had become darker in the shadow of the linden tree, a warm brown now, and he opened his mouth slightly. It smelled of fruit and alcohol, Frau Thamling's home-made fruit brandy from the stone bottle, which he had presumably drunk with the administrator when saying goodbye. 'You actually look like your sister,' he said in a low voice. 'Even lovelier, almost. Have you heard from her?'

The flywheel in the dairy had paused and she shook her head again and glanced out across the yard, where there was no one to be seen, just a few chickens sleeping in sandy hollows. It was so quiet that the rustle and creak of the reedbed in the sun could be heard, and she could feel Walter's heartbeat under her fingertips, more strongly the more firmly she pressed – as she did, to keep from trembling. He raised his eyebrows in surprise, and frowned at the same time.

He studied her for a long time, endlessly, it seemed to her, with a melancholy thoughtfulness, and she stepped closer to him, making him totter slightly too. Involuntarily he placed a hand on her waist, and now she could smell his hair-cream, as she had once on his pillow; it was the same one that her father had used. When she stood on tiptoes the pumps slipped from her heels. 'Hey, hey,' he muttered, 'what's this now?' He cleared his throat and sniffed; his voice remained hoarse. 'You're still a bit young, aren't you?'

She smiled seriously, and the tendril of hair fell back over her forehead. 'Am I?' she asked and stared awkwardly at his neckline, the sweat in the hollow of his throat. A bell rang out, metal clattered; someone cycled past them, but she didn't care. 'By the way it's my birthday tomorrow. At midnight, to be precise. Then I'll be thirteen.'

The vertical wrinkle above Walter's nose deepened. Again he gripped her hand and pulled her finger out of the round bullet hole, slightly frayed at the edges; one of the boot legs above them creaked in the heat, and everything in her sank. How could she have been so foolish as to tell him the number! In the moments before she had been age-less, like love; now, after a short, embarrassed glance at her hair and a painful twitch of the corners of his mouth, she was a child again.

He straightened the chain on her neck, the single pearl, and drew away from her with a gentleness that wounded her and brought tears to her eyes. At the same time she felt every freckle in her glowing face and heard him say, 'Well, then . . .' as if from a distance.

He kick-started the engine and put his foot on the accelerator, and looked almost relieved as he sat down on the broad saddle of the motorcycle. The exhaust clattered loudly, bluish smoke drifted through the shadow of the tree, a spiral flag, grey in the sun. 'Then I owe you a present!' he shouted and raised a hand in farewell, and rode slowly off across the ditch. 'I'll keep it for you!'

*

Motte walked with her as she brought the cooled buttermilk to the Klosterwald the next morning, under the chestnut trees. The nuns had been at work for hours, since lauds. They wore aprons over their habits, and some of them had rolled up their sleeves and wished her a happy birthday. Luisa took the two churns off her handlebars and set them down on Sister Mathilde's table. Surrounded by all kinds of tins, little bottles and tools, she was restoring a small panel showing two angels. Whoever they had once accompanied or protected – in their worm-eaten midst one could still make out the suggestion of a silhouette.

'Many happy returns!' she said, adding her congratulations to those of the others, and got to her feet to hug Luisa. The heavy fabric of her habit smelled of smoke, but behind it there was the aroma of a purity that had scarcely anything to do with soap. 'Thirteen! What an important age! At thirteen my hunch would have passed for a pair of wings. I had a dozen suitors, and I drove them all mad. Not with a swing of my hips of course, but . . .' She winked. '. . . with my head.'

Then she pointed to the campfire under the trees, where a charred pot steamed. 'There's lentil soup with shrimps; it should be ready any minute.'

She scratched the dog's throat and went back to work. She was scraping varnish and loose layers of paint from the votive painting, and mending cracks and holes in the wood with a paste, using a small, very pointed gooseneck spatula.

'Any news from the Red Cross? Did the tracing service get in touch?'

Shaking her head, Luisa looked out to the lake. A man stood in a boat, testing the bed with a long pole. The huts on the opposite shore had burned down, and the remains were still smoking. British soldiers with thick leather gloves were rolling up the barbed wire and pulling poles out of the peat. Some of their comrades, with cloths held in front of their faces, stood up to their shoulders in big trenches recovering the skeletons of the dead who had been buried there. Along the edges lay the sorted bones, piles of pelvises, ulnas, calf bones; hair still clung to some of the skulls. A soldier with a rusty canister on his back sprayed disinfectant over them, and Luisa turned away.

The nuns were singing quietly. A new roof had been put on the chapel, which had several ladders leaning against it; its half-timbering was freshly tarred and the spaces between them were currently being whitewashed. The words 'Non omnis moriar' were clearly carved above the door-post, and a novice with a white veil sat astride the roof adding new shingles to the little tower. The yoke for the bell was still empty.

'And what about the murder of that pilot?' Mathilde asked. 'There was that trial, wasn't there? Have they already sentenced your brother-in-law?'

Luisa nodded. 'He was taken to Flensburg, to the naval college, and shot in the basement. There won't be a grave.'

The nun raised her head and stared into the distance for a moment. 'God, how sad, in spite of everything. Should we pray for him?'

'No,' she said. 'He was a swine. I don't want to think about him any more. Or about my stepsister, that snake!'

The nun sighed. 'Oh come now . . . Practise forgiveness! Didn't she have a miscarriage?'

'Yes,' Luisa said and sat down on one of the wicker chairs at the table. 'But she's recovering already, I've heard. The Gauleiter has taken her on as a secretary.'

'Is that still his title?'

'I don't know. At any rate he's the same person, and he does a similar job – even though he was a member of the SS and murdered lots of Jews in Riga. The British think he's indispensable for administration and agriculture. He's the only one who can ensure a harvest.'

The nun grunted. 'Hmm, that's how things are and how they always will be. Or as the sage has it: You don't throw dirty water away if you have no clean water. They can all go to . . .'

She waved her hand through the air. Then she put on a pair of glasses, which enlarged her bright blue eyes, and opened a small notebook. Its pages were made of parchment, and when she lifted one, a circular piece of gold leaf gleamed beneath it. 'Pretty, isn't it? A nice British sergeant found it for me,' she said. 'A halo for a mere two Reichsmarks, if that isn't a bargain. Other people have to break their backs working for such things.'

The unadorned wooden cross which hung on a cord in front of her chest got in the way of her work; she threw it over her shoulder and onto her back. She applied some glue over the curly heads of the angels with the spatula, and Luisa shooed the dog away from the soup with a hiss. Then she pressed her cheek into her hand and asked, 'Sister Mathilde?' She cleared her throat. 'If you could be young again, would you still go into the convent?'

The nun looked up. 'What? Of course, child. Why do you ask?'

The girl shrugged. 'Just. I'm interested. Why did you become a nun in the first place?'

'Oh God . . .' She rummaged among the tools for a knife. 'I think one already is one, one just doesn't know it yet. But then one's eyes are opened. Wait a moment . . .'

The gold arched as she blew on it, then she pushed the knife underneath and lifted it from the page. 'My mother was an actress, a dicey profession at the end of the century.' She smiled. 'A beautiful actress doesn't need wages, theatre-owners thought in those days, and that meant: they're all whores anyway, they make more money in their sleep. Which she probably did. And when she fell pregnant she went back to her home, a small town in Bavaria, and the misery began.'

She applied some of the gold onto a faded halo and

pressed it down with the brush. 'A damp flat, poverty and sadness . . . She beat us children with wooden spoons, and of course there wasn't a trace of piety. But one winter evening she wanted me to go with her to her parents' grave – not an easy journey for a frail nine-year-old girl as I was at the time. The cemetery was on the other side of a hill, I coughed my lungs up on the steep rocky road and up at the top, where there was a statue of the mother of God, I became dizzy.'

She closed her eyes for a moment and breathed deeply. 'It was the beginning of November, and a wide wave of warm air blew towards me, a smell of smoking wicks and wax. In the whole huge graveyard that fell to the river, on every patch between the hedges and stones, lights were burning, a yellow and red flicker and glow, and the silhouettes of the many visitors stood out against it, and they stepped back with a whisper, like the souls of the dead. Never in my life had I seen such radiance, such a blaze in the night, you must know, and it was multiplied by the prism of my tears. I actually started crying.'

She applied some more gold around the hair of the other angel and dabbed it down, this time with her finger. 'That there might be another life beyond our wretched everyday, a world full of benevolence, beauty and elegance,' she went on, licking her fingertip, 'seemed to me like a miracle. Everyone was so mild-mannered, and I remember that my mother, with her hard mouth, suddenly seemed strange to me, that I no longer understood her bitterness and wondered why things were so cold and comfortless between us, when such bliss was possible, such a celebration of light. But she ignored my gaze. She leaned against the stone Madonna and took a pinch of snuff.'

The nun took a five-mark coin out of her dark brown habit, laid it on the halo and cut away the overhanging scraps of gold. 'At any rate, I knew at that moment that I was very close to the mystery, and planned to get even closer to it as quickly as possible.'

She looked with satisfaction over the rim of her glasses. 'Which is not to say that I didn't look very closely into all the things that I would have to give up. All those pretty boys . . . I was a wild one, believe me. I was your sister three times over.'

'And it wasn't hard for you to make that sacrifice?' Luisa asked.

She shook her head and looked at her watch. 'Well yes, at first, of course. I was twenty-two when I took my vow, and my first girlfriends were getting pregnant. But then again no, because actually there is no sacrifice, not really. If you overcome yourself and pure-heartedly give something of yourself that is dear to you or precious, once and for all, if you sacrifice it with conviction and without reserve, at that very second you receive a gift, do you understand? It's the only way!'

She smiled, and Luisa nodded, but in fact she had not the slightest idea what it might mean. But it was that very incomprehension that gave her the same sense of comfort as the feeling of printed letters under her fingers, even before a line has been read. Or like the thought of something good or delicious that one has saved for later. Motte stepped closer and laid his muzzle on her knees, and she scratched him between the ears, plucked a nettle from his fur and said, 'I would like to become a nun as well.'

Mathilde took off her glasses and looked at her in silence. A network of wrinkles and tiny warts surrounded her bright, shining eyes. With a shake of her head she took a cigarette from a Chesterfield box and tapped the mouth-piece firmly on the glass of her watch, and the mild seriousness in her expression made way for a silent sadness. 'Oh, child!' she said and struck a match. 'You're still so young. Wouldn't you rather experience something first?'

A vein pulsed under the pale skin on her wrist, the smoke floated over them in the still summer air and the dog yawned. As if cross-hatched by the slender beech trees on the shore, soldiers pushed a barrow full of bones to the gate, where a lorry waited. The roof slates of the chapel gleamed a watery grey in the sun, a new bell hung on the yoke, its clapper wrapped in paper. 'I've experienced every-thing,' Luisa replied.

The woman laughed, went over to the pot and lifted its battered lid. 'Well come on,' she said, 'have a bowl of soup first.'